M000028080

Behind the
FAKE Smile

Behind the Fake Smile
One Woman's Journey in Using Hellfire With Holy Water
Copyright © 2020 Jyl London. All rights reserved.

No part of this book may be reproduced, scanned, transmitted, or distributed in any form by any means, electronic or mechanical, including photocopying, recording, or by any information storage and retrieval system, without specific written permission from the publisher. The scanning, uploading, and distribution of this book via the Internet or via any other means without the permission of the publisher is illegal and punishable by law. Please purchase only authorized electronic editions, and do not participate in or encourage electronic piracy of copyrighted materials.

Please note that although the series is based on real-life and true stories, there are a few stories that have been fictionally dramatized for audience entertainment purposes only. The story is faithful to the author's experiences in the way that all creative nonfiction tries to recreate stories from memories as accurately as possible. The author has changed the characters' names to protect identities and privacy. Events, locations, and other details are assumed to be fictional. Nothing written should be assumed as an autobiography of the author's life.

Cover Design: Jyl London • Author Jyl London • www.jyllondon.com
Print & eBook Design: Dayna Linton • Day Agency • www.dayagency.com

ISBN: 978-1-7345981-0-0 (Paperback)
ISBN: 978-1-7345981-4-8 (Paperback)
ISBN: 978-1-7345981-1-7 (eBook)

Library of Congress Number: *Pending*

Printed in the United States of America

10 9 8 7 6 5 4 3 2 1

Behind the FAKE Smile

One woman's journey in using
hellfire with holy water

JYL LONDON

Introduction

DEPRESSION CAN'T HIT A moving target. That was a phrase to live by for Chelsea Hansen. She was full of life and love, and she had big goals. But soon she was to discover that life doesn't turn out the way she planned.

Behind the Fake Smile is a fictional book based on real-life experiences. It's the story of how Chelsea navigates a world of abuse, heartache, hurt, depression, disease, and loss. She discovers immense strength at a young age when she realized that no matter how many times she was knocked down, she found the willpower to get back up and smile another day.

It's a story of how ordinary people perform unknown miracles and give and receive signs that help them tackle their inner demons. It's about how people's hearts are touched and how that affects others through time and dimensions.

This book will penetrate your heart and soul as you experience life through Chelsea's cracked heart as she is guided through a journey of peace, love, and purpose. Ultimately, she learns how to get to the root of suffering and to replant it using hellfire with holy water.

Table of Contents

Chapter 1
FREDDY, THE BAD BOY, IS STILL A BAD BOY

*I*N A WORLD OF crazy chicks, just walk away, Chelsea
thought to herself, wondering why everyone in high
school was either crying or whining.

She could usually ignore it, but today it seemed as though
everyone was pulling her into the drama—especially her teammates, who were all fighting over boys and ruining their Friday
soccer game.

We are playing horribly. Nobody is focusing on the game,
Chelsea thought as she watched her teammates stop midfield to
dish out insults to one another.

After the game, her friend Teri walked up and gave Chelsea
a big hug, which surprised Chelsea. Teri was not really the hugging type and had rarely hugged Chelsea since their first meeting at a soccer camp months earlier. When they met, Chelsea

thought Teri was a short, stuck-up brat, her brown hair pulled so tight in a ponytail that Chelsea wondered if her hazel eyes would pop right out of her head. But later, Chelsea discovered that she had misjudged Teri's shyness as arrogance and now saw her as a tiny chihuahua on the field and a scared kitten off of it.

Chelsea looked at Teri and snorted. "Did it seem like I needed a hug?"

Teri nodded her head and giggled. "Well, you play well when you are annoyed, so I waited until after the game to do it. Sorry!"

They both giggled as Chelsea complained about how dramatic everyone was being and how their fighting was driving her crazy. Her parents were fighting with each other. Her sister Sadie was struggling with their parents. Her friends were fighting over boys, and now her teammates were fighting with each other. It was a lot to handle.

Teri and Chelsea hurried into the showers, and then Chelsea drove Teri to work.

The weekend had officially begun, but Chelsea felt like she wanted to run away and hide from life for a couple of days, even after her team's win.

My homework can wait tonight. I need to drive, Chelsea thought.

The best feeling for Chelsea was to drive and take in the world's beauty. The setting sun turned the rain clouds into luminous, red pillows as Chelsea drove up the mountain in her small town. She was mesmerized by the rain as it lashed her car. She pulled over to enjoy the sunset and her favorite playlist. The music and the chords burrowed deeper into her soul as she closed her eyes and listened to the lyrics. The melody comforted and grounded her as if she were hypnotized.

AT THE END OF Teri's shift, as promised, Chelsea arrived and sat impatiently, waiting for Teri in her car.

Tap! Tap! Tap! She looked over to see a guy at her window. He was about her height, but skinny with bloodshot green eyes. His blonde hair was longer and tousled like a surfer's.

She could see him mouth the words, "Roll down your window."

Chelsea cracked the window and said cautiously, "Yes?"

"I'm Teri's friend. Let me in," he commanded through the cracked window. Chelsea unlocked the car doors and motioned for him to sit in the passenger seat.

He was looking cocky with his long hair, ripped jeans, and a leather jacket. "Hey," he greeted, flipping the hair out of his eyes.

"Hey back," Chelsea retorted with a sarcastic smile.

He changed his tune a little after noting her tone. "I'm Freddy. I work with Teri, and I'm coming to tell you that she's running late and will be out in a bit. Ryder and Teri are still closing up."

Chelsea tilted her head and groaned at the delay.

"Don't worry, I'll keep you company," Freddy said.

Chelsea smiled, "Tell me about you. How long have you worked with Teri?"

Freddy blurted, "Well, I mainly work the day shift, so I don't see Teri that often at night. I was forced by the courts to work and pay off all my fines."

"I see. What did you do to have these work requirements and court fines?" Chelsea asked.

Freddy studied Chelsea's face and proceeded, "They were for drug and violence charges. I was in a bar selling drugs, and I got in a fight that put a man in the hospital."

Play it cool, Chels, your eyebrows are furrowing.

"In a bar, huh? So, I take it you're not in school like Teri and me," Chelsea said curiously.

"No, I don't go to school. It's hard enough to get to work since the courts took my driver's license away," Freddy sighed.

They continued to talk about his life and troubled past. As Freddy spoke, she noticed his demeanor was like an animal that has known intense suffering, such as a cautious dog that had been rescued from cruel indifferences. Right then, Chelsea knew he needed love and something steady to hold onto. He needed to be rescued from a hard life, and this intrigued her.

They were soon interrupted as Teri and Ryder came out of the store. Ryder was introduced as Freddy's best friend. Teri opened the front passenger door, and Freddy jumped out to allow her to sit down.

"Bye, girls," Freddy said, winking at Chelsea before sauntering away with Ryder. Chelsea noticed he kept looking back at her, and she gave him a small but genuine smile.

"Bye," she and Teri exclaimed as they pulled out of the parking lot.

Teri stated, "Thanks for coming to get me. Sorry, I'm late. I told Freddy to go and entertain you."

They were quiet for a second. "So, what do you think of Freddy?" Chelsea asked, trying to sound nonchalant and avoiding eye contact with Teri in case her look was disapproving.

"Well, he's definitely trouble, but fun," Teri said before giggling.

THAT NIGHT, CHELSEA COULDN'T stop thinking about Freddy. He wasn't her type. He was a complete train wreck, after all, but something was exciting about the idea of him she couldn't shake. She felt as though she knew him quite well already. Freddy told her about how his mom had him young and then cracked under the pressure of being a mom. Chelsea could sense that Freddy felt discarded and abandoned by most of the people in his life.

The phone rang, which startled Chelsea from her thoughts as her mom yelled, "It is for you, Chels!"

"Hello?" Chelsea answered.

"Well, hey," Freddy responded.

As they talked, Freddy continued describing his family and life more, Chelsea instantly felt like she wanted to prove to him that there are plenty of good people in the world, and she was one of them.

There is definitely a connection, or is it that I love that he is older? she thought as he was talking about his work and the hobby of building homes.

After hours of talking, Chelsea looked at the clock in a panic and said, "I still have to finish my homework. Can I talk to you later?"

"Homework on a Friday night?" Freddy laughed. "You *are* a goody goody. What girl hangs up the phone with a hot guy to do homework?"

Chelsea giggled, "Who said you were a hot guy? Have an amazing night, but I do have homework. I have soccer tournaments all weekend. Good night."

After she hung up, *Goody goody? I wonder if he really is a jerk or if that is part of his façade to protect himself.*

After an hour of homework, she put it on the nightstand and closed her eyes.

CHELSEA BEGAN WALKING ALONGSIDE a cliff, peering over the edge to see mountains peeking through the clouds. She felt cold and anxious.

"I need to get to the bottom of this mountain. I'm up way too high, and it's freezing," Chelsea muttered under her breath as she felt her teeth chatter.

She started to climb down the mountain, watching every step that she took to avoid falling. She put her hand down on a rock and felt a surge of pain in her finger. She looked over to see a rat nibbling on her hand. Its teeth were sharp and felt like she had been stabbed by a hypodermic needle. She smacked it away, and two other rats began climbing on her. They looked at her with their black beady eyes and...

BEEP! BEEP! BEEP! SHE was abruptly awoken by her alarm.

A WEEK LATER, CHELSEA came home bursting with energy. "Mom, Dad!" cried Chelsea enthusiastically as she entered the house. "Guess what?" she exclaimed as she ran into the living room where they were both glued to the television. "I made the high honor roll, and now I have two semesters with all As!"

Both of them looked at her, smiled, and then continued watching the game. Her excitement started to drop as she realized they were unresponsive to her news. She turned around and walked to her room, muttering to herself, "I swear, nothing I ever do is good enough."

Sadie gets all Ds and Fs, and they fuss over her. I get all As, and they say nothing to me. I'm so over it all! I'm going to call Jessica and see what she is doing tonight.

Jessica had been her best friend and soul sister since their first meeting in middle school. Chelsea couldn't shake that there was something about Jessica when they met, and she was right. They became instant best friends. Jessica was easy to talk to, and her hazel eyes sparkled as she spoke. Although Jessica was thin and quite attractive. She didn't play down her intelligence to play up her looks, like Chelsea. Chelsea loved that Jessica was 5'9", like her, and they were often asked if they were related, which always made Chelsea laugh. They didn't necessarily look alike, but their mannerisms did make it seem like they were related, but Jessica had lush blonde hair Chelsea envied. Chelsea had darker blonde hair, blue-green eyes, and the innocent-girl-next-door look. Nonetheless, Chelsea felt like it was the highest of compliments to be compared to Jessica.

Jessica answered the phone. "Hello?"

Chelsea said, "Hey, hot pants, let's go to the movies or something tonight."

Jessica sighed. "I can't. I have that dreaded family party. Why don't you come with and save me?"

Chelsea laughed. Right now, she could barely stand her own family. "Well, I love you, have lots of fun, but I don't want to be around *any* family."

Jessica giggled, and the two agreed to talk later.

Chelsea called Teri next, "Hi, Teri! What are you up to tonight?"

Teri replied, "Erica is coming to get me for a party. My family thinks it is a soccer thing, but it isn't. Want to come?"

"Deal, babycakes. I'm on my way over," Chelsea roared as she grabbed her shoes, put on more deodorant, and ran out the door.

"I'm going out!" she exclaimed to her family as the door was closing.

AT THE PARTY, TERI asked, "Want something to drink?"

Chelsea replied, "Nah, I'm good. I have only had a drink on two occasions before with my cousin. I don't want to be sick for our soccer game in the morning."

Teri laughed, "Oh, you will be fine. By the way, Freddy is on his way. Want a drink now?"

"Well, since you put it that way, I need a drink," Chelsea gasped as they laughed and talked about the upcoming soccer game.

Once Freddy and Ryder arrived with more alcohol everyone was drinking, except for Erica, who was refusing anything to drink and kept saying that she was the designated driver. Chelsea was rather impressed by Erica's response, given the heavy peer pressure that surrounded them. Chelsea, on the other hand, was definitely being swayed by the rebel, ex-drug user, and overall troubled young adult Freddy.

"Come on, Chelsea, one more drink," Freddy persisted as he shoved another beer can into her hands.

Just then, Teri rushed over and commanded, "We need to go. It's late, and we have a game in the morning." Teri was pulling Chelsea by the arm toward the door, almost ripping her shoulder out of the socket.

Freddy and Ryder followed behind, babbling, "We'll go with you guys! Chelsea, you can tell your mom you are staying over with Teri. After all, you have to wake up early for the game."

Chelsea wasn't ready to leave, and she liked the assertive Freddy.

My parents would hate him, she thought as he smoked a cigarette trying to look cool.

She looked at her friends, staggering out to the car as Freddy grabbed her hand, "I have a surprise for you."

Chelsea was never a huge fan of surprises, but this one she was curious about.

They all piled into the car and left the party. Erica stopped at a local park, waiting to ensure Teri's parents were in bed asleep before dropping them all back off drunk.

Freddy pulled Chelsea closer to him and gushed, "Ready for your surprise?"

Chelsea nodded as Freddy leaned in so far that he was almost on her lap as he gave her a big, wet kiss.

In her drunken haze, she decided to go with it. *He is a pretty good kisser.* She enjoyed knowing she wasn't the perfect little girl, or as Freddy would say, "a goody goody."

As they were kissing, Chelsea was startled by the sound of sirens and red and blue lights flashing behind them. She launched Freddy back into his own seat and blurted, "Get off me and put your seatbelt on."

The police officer came to the window and flashed a light through the window on them. The light blinded everyone in its wake.

"Ma'am, have you been drinking?" The police officer asked politely but suspiciously to Erica.

Erica shook her head and stuttered, "No."

"Please step out of the vehicle," the officer commanded as his partner watched everyone still seated in the car.

One by one, everyone was told to get out of the car and ordered to perform sobriety tests. Chelsea was concerned because she was failing all of the tests. *It is hard enough to walk in heels without alcohol, and now I have to stand on one foot.* She wobbled every time she tried.

"I need all of you to come with me," the officer said after it became clear that the group was underage and drunk.

ONCE CHELSEA ARRIVED HOME with her mom from the police station, she was met with a daggered stare from her dad, who demanded, "What were you thinking?"

Chelsea put her head down and replied, "The punch was spiked at the party, and now I don't feel good."

Like magic, both parents seemed appeased by her explanation, and she was allowed out of the room without further discussion.

In her bedroom, she was left thinking about what had happened. *I could hear Freddy being screamed at by the police officer all the way down the hall about his patrol. I hope he isn't in jail long.*

Chelsea then turned her thoughts about lying to her parents about the punch being spiked, but her life seemed too valuable to be killed over such a small, drunken mistake.

Chapter 2
A WOMAN AND HER DREAMS

———

CHELSEA WAS UP IN the mountains beneath a beautiful waterfall, swimming, and basking in the sun. She could hear the birds chirp as she felt the warmth of the sun on her face and shoulders. As she neared the edge of the swimming hole, she felt the rocks, pebbles, and sand underfoot. She looked over the edge of the cliff and saw another magnificent waterfall streaming down and crashing into a massive body of water below.

She could feel the current pulling her, so she started swimming rapidly in a different direction. The current became stronger and pulled her over the edge of the waterfall. She was free-falling until, with a *plop*, she was submerged into the body of water below. She swam quickly to the beachside, lifted herself up, and caught her breath.

The bright sun flashed through the trees onto the path of pebbles. Chelsea looked down to see she was surrounded by plumerias. She picked one up, smelled it, and began gathering them as she followed the path they were forming. She heard birds singing as a soft breeze blew on her face. As she continued to walk, she saw an older man with winter-white hair further down the road, holding a baby.

He peered up at her, smiled, and waved. She noticed his face was timeworn and wrinkled, but his eyes seemed to dance as he looked at Chelsea. He looked like an older version of her uncle, Jimmy. She wondered if it was her grandfather who had died when her mom was little. She had often pondered if he would be gentle and kind like her mom, or if he would be gruff and opinionated like her uncle. She began to walk over to find out whose baby he was holding—

Beep! Beep! Beep! She was abruptly interrupted by her alarm. She slammed the snooze button, hoping to return to her dream of waterfalls, plumerias, and loved ones, but after tossing and turning, she knew it was no use trying to go back to sleep. She turned off the alarm clock, stretched, and headed to the bathroom.

It was an icy day in October, the daylight was short, and the air was crisp. She had been dating Freddy for a few months and was meeting his friends and family for the first time. She wondered if her outfit would still be wrinkle-free after she had bundled it up, packing it with all of her books and soccer gear for the drive to school that morning.

On her way out the door, she saw her parents eating breakfast. Her mom buttered the toast while cooking eggs on the stove. Her dad was behind the newspaper, reading as he ate the toast as fast as her mom could prepare it. Chelsea's mom always put people before herself, especially when it came to taking care of her family. Her mom would often work ten hours and then come home and pamper her family. She was thin, with jet black hair and blue eyes that could see through to her soul. She was slightly shorter than Chelsea's 5'9" build and more petite than Chelsea's athletic and lean build.

Chelsea's mom saw her in the doorway of the kitchen and smiled. "Hi honey, do you want to come to eat something? I can hurry and make you an egg before school."

Chelsea shook her head, making her dangle earrings sway back and forth as she asked her parents, "You both coming to the game?" Chelsea's dad peered from the newspaper and winked as he nodded, and Chelsea's mom gave a sincere smile and stated, "Of course. We will be there."

Chelsea smiled back at them and then left the house as she felt her appreciation for them. They gave up a lot for her to play in all of her sports. She liked it when they made it to her games, even if her dad's yelling would sometimes be embarrassing to her. Chelsea's dad resembled a scary, grey-haired giant with his towering bulk. He bellowed when he laughed, and when he snored, the rooftop would lift from the house. His eyes were the same turbulent, depthless blue as the police uniform he wore.

She jumped into her car, suddenly nervous about the people she would meet at Freddy's family dinner and his friend's party later that night. She was curious to see what his family would be like because she had only heard stories about them from Freddy. Chelsea pictured his stepmom as a chubby, lazy woman with a house full of clutter and disarray. She then imagined his dad confrontational and staying at work as long as he could to avoid the children.

All of Chelsea's friends had met Freddy already, and so had her parents, though her parents certainly did not like the idea of the two dating. Chelsea's parents had always assumed the guy she was dating was from school, not a grown adult with no direction in life. They also knew Chelsea had to drive him everywhere for reasons she refused to say. Still, they were trying to be supportive in their own way, and Chelsea hoped Freddy's friends and family would have a more positive vibe and support for their relationship.

BEFORE THE PARTY, CHELSEA was invited to have dinner with Freddy's family. From Freddy's description, Chelsea believed his parents would be awful villains who abused him with a belt, never talked to him, and never helped him. But while everyone ate, Chelsea observed the family dynamics and concluded she liked them more than she had expected.

Freddy's parents took an interest in Chelsea and actively asked her questions. "Chelsea, Freddy says you are an all-star on your soccer team and that you have dreams to be a doctor one day."

Chelsea smiled and nodded. "Well, Freddy exaggerates. I play varsity high school soccer, but I wouldn't say I am an all-star.

I do have an awesome team that works well together, though. I do want to be a doctor and plan to move out of Utah the second I graduate from high school. I want to go to Stanford University and have my application ready to send next year. My grades and SATs are on track for a scholarship—I hope."

Freddy's parents looked at one another, and then Freddy's stepmom asked, "That is wonderful, Chelsea, you are so driven. I certainly didn't have goals like yours at the age of sixteen. You impress me."

Chelsea smiled and blushed a little.

From Freddy's parents, Chelsea learned that Freddy had nothing to do with his biological mother since she had remarried a few years prior. Freddy chimed in and indicated that his biological mom was a bitch and was a neglectful mom. As Freddy was describing his mom so nastily, it instantly made Chelsea upset. Chelsea's parents always taught her to show respect toward others, especially respect for elders. Freddy's words seemed undeserved based on the stories they were telling, which made Chelsea question Freddy's stories.

As the meal went on, Freddy's attitude and his constant talking over the top of his parents and the rolling of his eyes was making Chelsea more and more upset. She couldn't tolerate Freddy's disrespect toward his parents. She tried to change the subject.

Chelsea looked at Freddy's parents and asked, "How did the two of you meet?"

Freddy's stepmom talked about how they were set up on a blind date. "I didn't know if I wanted to date someone with children—"

Freddy chimed in. "I struggled when she moved into the house."

Chelsea smiled and asked Freddy inquisitively, "Is it because you felt like you were getting replaced? Why would you struggle when your dad remarried?"

Freddy's stepmom replied, "I was stricter than what he was used to."

Freddy interjected again as he looked at Chelsea with pride and sneered, "I ran away from home and lived on the streets. I then got into drugs." He paused before continuing, "I wanted my life back to how it was before my dad got married. In my drug-induced haze, I had an elaborate plot to kill my stepmom. I almost executed it when I was picked up by the police for the bar fight that I told you about."

Chelsea's head was spinning. *You planned to murder your stepmom? That is so beyond messed up. He seems like he is proud of it instead of ashamed of it.*

AFTER DINNER, FREDDY AND Chelsea were driving alone to the party. Freddy could tell Chelsea was upset when he tried to grab her hand, but she smacked his hand away. Freddy bugged her on what was wrong until she snapped, "You know, I don't know the whole situation with your bio mom, but I am not impressed hearing you call her a bitch over and over, and I definitely wasn't impressed about you retelling, with pride, your plans to murder your stepmom. I'd rather not hear that shit from you. Have some class, for hell's sakes."

Freddy sighed as he held up his hands like he was under arrest and promised, "I'll work on it, Babe."

She was driving, lost in thought, and she had a sick feeling that the night wasn't going to end well. She was interrupted from her thoughts as Freddy screamed abruptly, "Turn here!"

The tires squealed as she rounded a tight corner, nearly hitting a parked car. The car started sliding on the ice and gravel. She looked up to see another parked vehicle in front of her that she was going to hit head-on. She cranked the wheel hard to try and avoid it. Almost like it was in slow motion, she saw the front of her car crunch against it before her head bashed into the windshield, and everything went black.

WHEN SHE AWOKE, THE horn was blaring, and the soundtrack kept playing the same verse over and over, "You Oughta Know." She grabbed her head with one hand and looked at the other hand to see it covered in blood. Her chest was caved in as if her shoulders were unable to move back, and she struggled to breathe.

She looked over to see Freddy's arm gushing and spurting blood everywhere. She couldn't see his face under all the blood. She shook him to wake him up, but he didn't respond. She grabbed her jacket and tied it around his arm, hoping to stop the bleeding. She pried her car door open and ran to the nearest house. The home was across the street, but to Chelsea, it felt like she was running for hours, struggling for every breath she took.

Her fists pounded on the neighbor's door. A woman opened the door to find Chelsea crying, screaming for her to call 911.

The lady looked at her with suspicion and asked, "Is this a Halloween joke?"

Chelsea pointed to the cars behind her, which looked like two cars molded into one.

The lady quickly apologized. "I'll call now. I'm so sorry. I've never seen that much blood."

Chelsea rushed back to her car and began putting pressure on Freddy's face and arm to stop the bleeding.

"God, I know I have not been the best lately, but please save him," Chelsea pleaded over and over. She felt herself wanting to sleep but resisted for fear of leaving Freddy.

She heard the sirens and knew help had arrived. The paramedics, police, and fire department showed up almost simultaneously. She looked over and could see two paramedics put Freddy on a gurney and into an ambulance. A couple of paramedics rushed to her side. They helped her onto a stretcher and wheeled her into the ambulance. Now that she was lying down, she surrendered to sleep.

CHELSEA FELT WARM LIKE the sun was dusting her nose with more freckles as she walked through the flowers on her way to see her grandpa sitting on a bench in the meadow. She arrived, and he handed her the baby. She looked down and smiled, asking whose baby it was, but he never said a word. She studied the baby's little face, the perfect bridge of her nose, her tiny lips, and her bright eyes until Chelsea felt every part of her was committed to memory. She smiled as she looked over at her grandpa. He continued to watch Chelsea fawn over the baby.

Everything felt familiar and happy. Chelsea could feel love like she had never known it before. She turned around and saw a man surrounded by a bright light. She got up from the bench and walked over to the glowing man. She felt pure happiness, love, and warmth in his presence. He opened his arms to Chelsea, and she handed him the perfect baby.

"CHELSEA? CHELSEA? WAKE UP, Chelsea. How are you feeling?" The nurse asked, pulling Chelsea from her dreams. Chelsea felt groggy and in a daze. She opened her eyes to see a blurry white room. She could smell the strong aroma of aseptic mixed with latex. It took a few moments before her brain registered what had happened, and she instantly panicked as she asked, "How is Freddy?"

The nurse touched her shoulder and said, "You are both going to be fine. You were both lucky on this one. You lost a lot of blood."

"Can I go and see him?" Chelsea asked. The nurse nodded as she helped Chelsea get into a wheelchair and rolled her down a few doors into his room.

When they arrived at the room, he was already alert and talking to his parents. She felt a sudden relief come across her.

She grabbed his hand and kept repeating her apology until he smiled at her.

He squeezed her hand. "It is okay. How are you?" Chelsea looked up from her wheelchair at the nurse.

The nurse explained, "She lost a lot of blood and has a concussion, like you. She does have broken ribs and a cracked sternum."

Chelsea's parents came rushing into the room. Her mother immediately hugged her tight.

The nurse smiled and suggested, "Let's get her back into bed."

When they were back in her hospital room, Chelsea asked her mom, "Do you have a photo of grandpa? I continually see him in my dreams."

Her mother said in shock, "Of course—we will get out the photo albums when we get home." She gently brushed the hair from Chelsea's face in a soft, soothing way as she helped Chelsea lay back further in the bed. "What was he doing during the dream?"

"He handed me a baby, but then God took the baby from me," Chelsea explained as her eyes grew heavy.

"Do you always have these types of dreams, Chels?" her mother asked while raising her eyebrows and looking at her husband.

"I always dream about plumeria flowers," Chelsea said as her eyes closed shut despite her attempts to keep them open.

"Why don't you rest, honey?" her dad whispered. Chelsea fell back to sleep as though she was under a spell.

IT WAS A COUPLE of weeks after the car accident, and Chelsea healed quickly. She marveled at how her body healed after all her injuries and surgeries. Chelsea looked down at her knee, remembering when she had seen the bone through the flesh in the hospital. She remembered that her favorite jeans were cut off at the knees as the paramedics stopped the oozing blood. Gently, she touched the stitches and the bluish-purple bruise forming around it. *That's gonna scar, but at least it is healing,* she thought as her phone rang.

"Hello?" she said.

Freddy insisted, "Be ready in fifteen minutes. I'm coming over, and don't say you're doing homework. It can wait."

She chuckled, "Well, all righty, Mr. Bossy. How are you going to get here?"

He sighed, "I have us a driver. Go get ready and wear something warm. Be ready to have your heart race. I love you, Chels."

Minutes later, there was a knock at the door, and Chelsea bounced out and into Freddy's arms as she gushed, "Where are we going?"

Freddy laughed, "We're going to dinner first at your favorite sushi restaurant."

Chelsea's lips lifted upwards into a huge smile, "You're going to have sushi with me? Freddy, you hate sushi. That's true love."

Freddy hugged her and lifted her up in the air. His eyes looked up to her as he exclaimed, "Tonight is all about spending time with you and only you."

"Aw, you're a smooth talker," Chelsea said, jumping in the car as he opened the door for her.

Freddy hugged her and rubbed her shoulders as he sang to her. She felt the love in his heart and the tenderness of his touch. She wished the moment would never end when the car came to a stop at the restaurant.

Freddy held Chelsea's hand as he escorted her inside. It was a grand space with the lights turned down, tiny candles flickering as though they were dancing to the music.

Freddy studied Chelsea's face, almost as if he were making a portrait in his head, as he said, "You are the best thing that has ever happened to me. My life has completely changed, and I owe it all to how kind and loving you are."

She smiled and stood up from the table and kissed him.

On their car ride after dinner, Chelsea felt like her heart was beating so hard that it might fall out of her chest. Her mind feared that her heart was taking control of her emotions. She had never experienced a love like the one she had with Freddy. He adored her and was showing it more each day. The car stopped, and he kissed her hand as he intertwined his fingers with hers.

Chelsea looked up as they were getting out of the car and laughed, "A haunted house? You realize I am a chickenshit, right?"

Freddy snorted, "I know, but this guarantees that you will hold onto me and hug me the entire time. When I said the night was all about you, I meant the sushi. This part is all about me. I'm going to have the hottest girl all over me tonight."

Chelsea playfully smacked his shoulder as she crawled inside his jacket and giggled, "I certainly will be all over you tonight. Well played, Freddy, well played."

Chapter 3
TIME FOR A CHANGE

"COME ON, CHELSEA, YOU need to have shots with us! It is New Year's Eve, after all," Freddy said, utterly wasted.

Chelsea had told her parents she was spending the night at Teri's house, celebrating with a bunch of friends. Most of that story was true, except she didn't mention that the "hoodlum guy," as her dad referred to Freddy, was going to be there.

"Alright, I'll do it," Chelsea told him as she smiled and took her glass.

The night was filled with playing drinking games and dancing. Chelsea laughed as she saw her friends dancing. *They are so silly*, she thought as she danced with Freddy.

Chelsea grabbed her friend, Dottie, to come and dance with them, but Dottie didn't know the steps. Freddy grabbed

Dottie's hand and helped her learn the dance. Chelsea smiled as she left to get the camera. Freddy didn't know that Dottie was also Chelsea's student she tutored from a special needs group.

Chelsea marveled as she watched Freddy and Dottie. *He acts like a tough guy, but he has a soft heart. I'm sure he noticed that she is a little slower, but he is so patient with her. She endures a lot of bullying, and him being kind to her says a lot about his character.*

Teri asked Chelsea to join in a game of truth or lie. Chelsea had never played the game before, but it looked like they were all having fun. Teri explained the rules: "You have two minutes to tell an embarrassing story, and we need to guess if it is the truth or a lie. If someone guesses wrong, they have to take a shot."

Ryder was seated and began to tell his story, "I was picking a girl up for a first date—a blind date. The girl, Lisa, was gorgeous with long blonde hair, a smoking-hot body, and lips that made you want to kiss them. Lisa was still getting ready when I arrived to pick her up. I sat on the couch, waiting when my nerves started to act up."

He paused as he stood up. "You know what I'm talking about. Your stomach grumbling loudly like it's yelling at you to go to the bathroom. I went into the bathroom down the hall. I pooped so much that when I flushed, it clogged the toilet and started to overflow."

Ryder was gesturing with his hands as he talked, "I searched everywhere for a plunger, but I couldn't find one. The toilet kept overflowing as poop lodged at the bottom. I looked around in panic as I saw the white marble flooded with toilet and poop water. My shoes and pants were wet, and I finally yelled to her, 'Lisa? Do you have a plunger?' Lisa came barreling out of her bedroom to the bathroom. She looked at me, the overflowing toilet, and the flooded bathroom floor and burst out laughing. She gave me a plunger, and while she finished getting ready, I cleaned the bathroom. The entire date, I couldn't make eye contact with her because I knew that she had seen my poop log that clogged her toilet. Needless to say, we didn't have a second date."

Everyone in the circle looked at each other, nodding their heads. One by one, those in the circle said over and over, "True."

Ryder laughed and said, "It was false."

Chelsea laughed and took a shot, saying, "You suck, Ryder. That is a hell of a story to be false."

Teri punched Ryder on the arm, "Smartass!" Then she looked at Chelsea and said, "Alright, Chels, it is your turn."

Chelsea took a moment to think. She stood as she explained, "There was this boy, Justin, and I had the biggest crush on him in middle school. On the last day of school, we all got together to celebrate at a local waterslide. Justin was flirting with me, and I was flirting back. As we were going up to the top of the waterslide, Justin hopped in front of me and said, 'I'll go first and show you how to do it.' I watched him go head-first down the waterslide."

Chelsea stopped as she looked at everyone listening to her story. Teri had wide eyes, Ryder was gulping his drink, and the others were listening intently. She continued, "I decided to follow his lead and dove head-first down the waterslide. I screamed the whole way down. Water sprayed in my eyes and went inside my nose, and I felt like I had drunk at least my water supply for the day."

She made eye contact with everyone in the circle as she recounted, "I plopped into the pool at the end. I popped out of the water, smiling because I had shown him that I could be just as brave and go down that huge slide head-first too. Justin was right there waiting for me. He was looking hot with his wet hair and his chest glistening with the water and sunlight. He looked at me and gasped. I wondered if he was impressed or scared because I had makeup running down my face."

Chelsea paused as she took a deep breath, "People were looking at me and pointing. Justin stood there with his mouth hanging open. I looked down to see that my bikini top was no longer on my body. I covered myself with my hands and sank back into the water. Secretly, I was hoping that I would drown. Justin found my bikini top and gave it to me. He stood in front of me as he helped me put it back on. My face was bright red, my hair was dripping, and my eyes were wide open in shock and mortification. Justin went to say something and stopped as he realized both of his hands were still on my chest. And that, my dear friends, was my first experience having a boy see my boobs."

People finally quit laughing and unanimously said, "True."

Teri snorted, "Well, Chels, if you don't want us to know it is true, you need to hide your emotions and body language better. You blushed the entire time you told that story."

Chelsea chuckled, "It was the only embarrassing story I could think of, but like Ryder in his story, I always struggled to look Justin in the eye after that."

AFTER A FEW HOURS of dancing and drinking, Chelsea's head was spinning. She felt like she could barely stand up or even sit up straight. She looked at everyone with her eyes half-open as she watched them spin with the room. "I need to lie down. I don't feel well," she slurred. She stumbled down the hall, holding on to the walls to keep from falling. She found Teri's bedroom and plopped down to lay on the bed.

She was asleep within seconds, but the sound of the door opening woke her up.

"Baby, are you okay?" Freddy asked from the doorway.

She didn't answer, instead turned over to avoid the dim light entering through the opened door.

Freddy came into the room and shut the door behind him. He then crawled into bed next to Chelsea and began to cuddle her. For a moment, she felt better as he held her close. It was nice to think he cared when she felt so sick. However, that feeling disappeared as he started to kiss her and murmured, "Oh, you poor thing, do you need anything?"

"I need sleep," she groaned. "I don't feel good."

Chelsea felt everything around her spin. It didn't even help when she buried her head in the pillow under her. She thought Freddy would leave her to rest longer, but she felt him rise slightly and climb atop her. He kissed her neck.

She pushed his face away and buried her face in the soft pillow beneath her head, but he continued to touch her and lifted up her dress. His hands made their way up to her chest as he grabbed between her legs at the same time. He was groaning and moaning on top of her.

She was disgusted. She wanted Freddy to stop, and she kept telling him so.

"Stop! I don't feel good," she told him over and over, pushing at his arms when she could gather a little strength, but he wasn't deterred.

He continued to kiss her, and she could taste the combination of smoke and alcohol, which made her feel even sicker. She was trying to move but felt paralyzed with fear. The entire room was spinning, and he had her pinned down. She felt pain and shock as he touched her. She tried to twist away in the bed, but he stopped her from getting more than half a foot away. As she tried to tell him to stop again, he hushed her and covered her mouth. He pulled her back underneath him and whispered, "It is okay—I'll be gentle."

He unzipped his pants, spread her legs open, and thrust himself inside her.

It hurt, and she cringed. It felt like a pit had opened in her stomach, and she wanted to throw up.

He was moving up and down, thrusting into her while grunting.

After a couple minutes, she heard a loud, final grunt from him before he rolled off of her and took deep breaths as though he had run a mile in six minutes. He kissed her forehead, dressed, and walked out of the room while she lay there frozen in horror.

Chelsea's head was spinning, her stomach hurt, and her dress was pulled up in disarray.

Why would he have sex with me and then leave the room? She scrambled to pull herself together. She pulled her dress down and found her underwear near the foot of the bed.

She felt cheap, used, and alone as she heard fireworks going off outside.

THE NEXT MORNING, CHELSEA was lying on the bathroom floor. Teri knocked and walked in. "Are you okay? You have been crying and throwing up all morning."

Chelsea laid on the cold tile and groaned. "I am heartbroken and hungover."

Teri looked at Chelsea, confused. "I'm hungover too, but what do you mean heartbroken? It seemed like you and Freddy were having an amazing time."

Chelsea nodded and then sobbed uncontrollably. "Teri, I felt sick, so I went into your room and, um—" Chelsea blew her nose and wiped the tears from her eyes as she continued, "He came in the room, and I told him to stop, but he kept kissing me. Um—he then pinned me down and had sex with me."

Teri's eyes were wide as she listened to Chelsea and then asked, "What are you going to do? He raped you."

Chelsea looked at her through the tears. "I don't know. I thought he loved me, but that didn't feel like love. It all felt like a blur, but I did tell him to stop several times. I'm in shock that he would do that."

As she recalled the night, Chelsea felt a strength rise up within her. "I'm not going to talk to him again. I am sixteen years old, and I can't have a guy who wants me to drink and have sex with him. A guy who leaves me sick and alone after taking my virginity."

Teri hugged her, moving the tear-drenched hair out of her face and whispered, "It will be alright, Chels, it will be alright. Freddy did not deserve you. He took advantage of you. I am so sorry."

A MONTH WENT BY, and Jessica pulled Chelsea out of bed. Jessica demanded, "Chels, you are going to get out of bed. I am worried about you. I know you are heartbroken, but going home every night and back to bed is not healthy. Your eyes are puffy, and your room is a mess. None of this is like you. If I have to drag you out every single day, then I will, but I am not going to let you wallow any longer. Freddy was your first love, but he won't be your last love. I'm proud of you for avoiding Freddy's phone calls and not seeing him for so long. Freddy has been persistent, I'll give him that, but he doesn't deserve you to give him a chance."

Jessica paused and said with a smirk, "What about that hot and sweet guy, Travis? He has asked you out for months."

Chelsea smiled and sighed. "I know you are right. I swear I am getting stronger every day, but I am still in shock about Freddy. I really loved him, and he broke my heart. And yes, I should go out with Travis. If anything, he is good eye candy."

TRAVIS WAS THRILLED CHELSEA agreed to go out with him. He went all out, with a fancy candlelit dinner and a dozen roses. Travis was a gentleman to Chelsea as he opened doors and listened intently to her dreams. He actively listened as she would beam about becoming a doctor. He took her out on dates and didn't rely on her to drive him everywhere. Plus, her parents liked him, but to Chelsea, he wasn't exciting. Still, he was nice, and she wanted nice.

On their one-month anniversary, Travis took Chelsea to a restaurant near the movie theater they were planning to visit later that night. While Chelsea was enjoying the meal, the conversation had turned a little too dull, and she started to wish something exciting would happen to liven up the night.

Her hopes were answered as Freddy walked into the restaurant. He saw her before she saw him, and he stormed across the dining room, making a beeline for their table. He grabbed Chelsea by the arm and hissed, "Get up—we need to talk."

Chelsea, in shock, didn't move. He hardly seemed to notice her because he was glaring at Travis, who looked like a frightened puppy.

Chelsea stuttered to say something, but before she could get a single word out, Freddy dragged her out of her seat and outside with a forceful pull.

Once outside in the parking lot, Freddy released Chelsea's arm.

He paced back and forth while he yelled, "You tramp! You're dating someone else? You know I love you!"

Chelsea, taken back by his hostility, scolded, "Look, let's talk later. I promise I will hear you out. I have questions for you too, but you can't barge into a restaurant and drag me out."

He stopped pacing and looked at her like she had sprouted a second nose. She huffed at him before turning around as she stormed back into the restaurant.

Travis tried to pretend like the whole thing never happened when she came back in, which somehow infuriated Chelsea more than Freddy's outburst in the parking lot.

They never made it to the movie. Chelsea had had enough and wanted to go home.

CHELSEA WAS LOST IN thought about Freddy and couldn't sleep. She looked at her phone to see it was only 9 P.M. and saw she had a missed call and voicemail. She pressed play and heard, "Chels, baby. I will always love you. I know we couldn't work, and I am sorry for that. It was all my fault. I wanted you to know I am eternally thankful for you. The example you were to me and to everyone around you. You are an amazing person, and I left your life in total disarray. Please know that I love you, and my life will never be the same without you. You have broken me, and I love you more than I can explain on this voicemail."

The heartache swirled unrestrained in Chelsea's chest as her head swam with half-formed regrets. She felt her melancholy mood hang over her like a black cloud. She couldn't take not talking to Freddy any longer, and she picked up the phone and called him. "Let's meet up and talk."

"I'm with Ryder and Teri tonight. You could join us. There is a party at Ryder's place. We'll come and pick you up in fifteen minutes. Does that work?" Freddy asked, and Chelsea agreed. She was surprised Teri was still friends with Freddy, but then again, she felt conflicted about Freddy, too. Besides, with Teri there, knowing what had happened, Chelsea felt a little safer going out with Freddy again.

At the party, Freddy grabbed Chelsea's hand and took her outside.

"I am sorry for leaving you when you were sick. I love you," he told her.

"I felt completely used and alone," Chelsea snapped.

"I know, baby," he said, looking guilty. He continually apologized as Chelsea listened with crossed arms and heavy glare. As he spoke, she couldn't help feeling the same flutters of excitement and giddiness she felt with him before the New Year's Eve party.

Maybe it really was a drunken mistake.

"I will never feel like that again. If I do, I have no problem dating other people," she demanded, folding under the internal pressure to forgive him. Freddy smiled and nodded his head.

"I'm sorry, Chels. I will never do it again," he said over and over as he hugged her and kissed her.

They both returned to the party. They were all drinking and laughing. Chelsea kept turning down drinks after her second one and explained, "Oh no, I did that months ago, and it didn't end well."

The group laughed at her and continued to offer as the night went on.

"Stick to one type, and you'll be fine. No tequila! Here, try this," Ryder said as he made her a drink. It was a sweet drink with rum. It didn't even taste like alcohol, so she figured it must not have much alcohol in it.

By the time she was close to finishing Ryder's concoction, she had started feeling like she was getting whirly again, and the room started spinning. She went looking for Teri to drive her home but found Teri to be equally drunk as her, if not more.

She turned to Freddy. "I need to go home."

Freddy went and talked to Ryder, who gave him his keys. Freddy then accompanied Chelsea out to Ryder's truck. He helped her in before he hopped into the driver's seat.

"I thought you didn't have your license?" she asked suspiciously.

"I got it back," he told her as they pulled out of the driveway.

They were both quiet as he began driving toward her house. Halfway there, she started to feel better. *Maybe I just needed fresh air,* she wondered, and she began to sing and tease Freddy.

Freddy chuckled, "It looks like someone is feeling better."

Chelsea snickered. "Looks like I needed fresh air."

Freddy pulled into a local park and stopped. "Let's go in the truck bed and look at the stars. Ryder has a mattress, blankets, and a battery heater."

They gazed up at the stars, naming the constellations and laughing about events at the party. He leaned over, pulled her in close, and kissed her.

She had missed the comfort of him cuddling her and the warm, safe feeling from his company.

Under the night sky, he touched her again, but this time, it felt different. She felt different. As he touched her, she began to heat up and wanted to get even closer to him, yearning and moaning at his touch. *Why the hell not? I already lost my virginity.*

As he started to undress them both, she helped.

"You do have protection, right?" she asked as their clothes were coming off. He dug into the pockets of his discarded jeans and pulled a condom out. He showed her the shiny silver square before opening it and rolling it on.

AFTER THEY FINISHED, SHE felt happy. It wasn't just sex. They had made love, and she felt close to him. They cuddled afterward and talked. The sex wasn't even close to the same experience she had before.

He dropped her off at her house an hour later. When she climbed into bed, she looked up at her ceiling and listened to love songs, realizing she felt peace and happiness. As she began drifting to sleep, she knew it was peace and happiness with herself, not Freddy.

I'm gonna end things permanently with Freddy in the morning. She stared at her ceiling, eyes growing heavy. *I'm way too young, and I need to follow my dreams. Tonight was lovely, and I do love him, but I can't be what I want with him.*

She continued to contemplate her decision. "I need a guy who will support my dreams," she mumbled out loud to reassure herself as her mind was in a carousel of thoughts. Every idea, every notion commanded analysis before she could go to sleep. She reached into her nightstand and grabbed her journal. With each stride of the pen, her mind became clearer and more resolute. She closed her eyes and took a deep breath and steeled herself to only think of her future. She put the journal away and drifted to sleep.

Chapter 4
CAN'T ZIP UP MY FAT PANTS

—————

"**O**H, MY HELL, JESSICA, I am getting fat. These pants will not zip up. I need to go to the track and run more," said Chelsea frantically as she tried to find a single pair of pants that would fit her growing hips.

Jessica laughed, "Maybe you're bloating more and retaining water. I heard it can happen during your period." Jessica picked up a pair of pants that looked forgotten in the corner of Chelsea's closet and tossed them onto Chelsea's "try on next" pile.

"Seriously, I'm going running now," Chelsea insisted when the next two pairs didn't fit either. She grabbed some sweats and slipped them on while Jessica jumped onto the bed.

"Why is it that when I am happy without guys, I get fat?" Chelsea asked.

"You're not fat!" Jessica exclaimed, grabbing Chelsea's arm and pulling her onto the bed. Chelsea collapsed next to Jessica, groaning.

"I've run like a thousand miles this week, and I'm still not losing any weight, Jess," Chelsea said. Jessica nodded, listening as Chelsea talked.

Chelsea was an avid, fast runner with a lean body. She loved running when she had the track all to herself, but now the amount of time spent running was getting ridiculous, especially with little results.

———

It was President's Day weekend. The air was crisp, and the skies were crystal blue. Chelsea could see the snowcapped mountains in the distance as she looked out the window and saw Jessica's car pull into the driveway.

They were planning something low-key for Chelsea's birthday. After they were done talking about the birthday plans, Jessica asked, "What's up with Freddy? Anything new happening?"

Chelsea laughed. "He is so dramatic! Last time he called, he accused me of dating Travis again. He was mean and swore at me, so I hung up."

Jessica laughed, too. "Men always assume we break up for another man. It blows their mind to think that we break up because they no longer fit in our life."

Chelsea then explained she wasn't feeling well on her run earlier that morning.

"Maybe you're pushing yourself too hard on these runs. I mean, you have been going at it a lot lately," Jessica said, concerned.

Chelsea shook her head. "Maybe I'm getting the flu?"

Jessica thought about it for a second and shook her head. "No, the flu wouldn't last this long. Besides, you're not sneezing or coughing." Chelsea nodded in agreement.

"What else could it be, though?" Chelsea wondered aloud. The two sat in silence for a few moments, thinking.

"You don't think you could be pregnant, do you?" Jessica questioned.

Chelsea burst into laughter. "We only had sex twice, and I haven't missed a period. Besides, the second time, we used protection. I've had a few periods since the first time."

"Maybe we should go and buy a pregnancy test just to make sure," Jessica suggested. "Do you feel good enough to escape and go to the store?"

Chelsea smiled and grabbed her keys.

AT THE DRUG STORE, they bought a pregnancy test and snacks to eat later. They went into the bathroom at the store, and Chelsea peed on the test stick.

In a few short minutes, they saw two faint, pink lines appear. Chelsea felt her stomach drop, and the world crumbled underneath her feet as she stared at the little lines.

"Oh, my God, Jess!" Chelsea exclaimed, clutching the stick and shaking. "What should I do?"

Chelsea panicked and felt a cold sweat come over her body as she looked down at the pregnancy test again.

"Calm down," Jessica said, holding onto Chelsea's shoulders. "Drug store tests aren't always accurate. We need something more solid."

She encouraged Chelsea to take a deep breath and had her sit back down on the toilet seat. Jessica started pacing around the bathroom to clear her head and think while Chelsea tried not to panic again.

"There's this nonprofit clinic right by the college. You can pee in a jar and take it in anonymously to get the test results. I'm sure you aren't pregnant, but that would be more accurate than a cheap stick," Jessica soothed as she stopped pacing.

Chelsea nodded as she stated, "I have a friend, Misty, who goes to that college. Maybe she could help."

"Yeah!" Jessica declared. "Call Misty to see if she would take the sample there on her way to the college next week."

As soon as they arrived back at Chelsea's house, they made the call to Misty, who reluctantly agreed.

CHELSEA FELT AS THOUGH her organs were in a storm by the way her emotions were swirling around in her body. She was too scared to know if she was pregnant. Knowing meant she'd have to pretend she was going to be alright when in her gut, she knew that she wouldn't be okay. She reluctantly peed in a jar and waited anxiously at the high school for Misty to pick it up on her way to college. Chelsea saw Misty's white car come skirting into the parking lot and ran out to meet her.

"I'm sure it is nothing, but thank you for doing this, Misty." Chelsea reassured, but fidgeted due to feeling so awkward about the whole situation. Misty smiled at her and gave her a hug before she jumped back into her car and drove away.

Chelsea slipped back into her regular routine in school. In class, she sat watching the clock and praying for it to speed up so she could eat lunch. The phone in her classroom rang.

"Um, yes, I'll send her right down," the teacher said after answering it.

"Chelsea Hansen, you are being paged to the front office," he stated to the class. "Take your things with you."

Everyone oohed and aahed as the straight-A student gathered her things to leave. When she walked into the office, she greeted the office assistant and informed her she had been paged.

The office assistant led her into an empty office. "Chelsea, you have a call on line four," she said as she pointed to the phone before exiting the room.

Chelsea picked up the phone and pressed the flashing button. "Hello?"

"Hi, Chels, it is Misty. They won't tell me anything, and they need you to come and get the results of the pregnancy test," Misty urged.

"Okay, I'll head over as soon as possible," Chelsea sighed. Then she checked herself out of school, ran to her locker, and drove to meet Misty at the clinic.

UPON ARRIVAL, BOTH SHE and Misty were pulled into a counseling room. After a few minutes of waiting, a woman walked in. She was wearing a white coat, her hair was styled up in a bun, and she had dark eyes.

She handed Chelsea a pink piece of paper. "Your test results are positive. I see you are fairly young, so let me present all your options and give you some things to think about."

"Wait, what? How are they positive? That means I am pregnant, right? But I can't be pregnant," Chelsea stammered.

The doctor made a pursed, teeth-sucking sound before standing up and moving to the chair next to Chelsea's. The doctor touched her shoulder and consoled her. "Yes, you are pregnant. It is 99% positive that you are pregnant."

Chelsea stood up, shaking, holding the papers tightly, and crumpling the edges in her grip.

"I can't believe it's positive," she cried, looking into the doctor's eyes, and then she stood up and began pacing the room. "How is that possible? Like, really—how is it possible? We wore protection, and it was only two times a month apart," Chelsea rambled.

The doctor encouraged her to sit back down. As she did, Misty rubbed her back, but it didn't help sooth, Chelsea.

"This makes no sense. I've had periods since then. We aren't even dating anymore. Oh, my God! What am I going to do?" Chelsea pleaded.

She looked over to see Misty shaking her head, her eyes wide open, looking confused and concerned. The doctor sat with her hands on her knees, smiling, with her head cocked to one side. She was trying to sympathize with Chelsea's rambling.

"Well, there are a few options. There is adoption, abortion, or you can keep the baby. Here are some pamphlets for you to read to help you understand all of your options," the doctor explained as she stood up and headed toward the door. On her way out, the doctor said, "I'll leave you alone to process the information. Once you are ready, come out and schedule an appointment with the front desk."

She grabbed the chart attached to the door and closed the door, leaving Chelsea and Misty alone.

Chelsea stared at Misty and was shaking her head in disbelief, dismay, and absolute disgust. Her eyes were fighting back the tears. She quickly hugged Misty and sobbed, "I can't process this right now. I have to go back to school."

THE REST OF THE day went by in a blur for Chelsea. She made it back to school but was too overwhelmed to focus. She was confused and scared, and she knew her future was going to be drastically different than what she had imagined. It didn't make sense to her.

Out of all of her friends, she was the only one not actively having sex, and she had only had sex two times. He used protection. She had dumped him because she would not let him keep her in the state that she never felt was home. Freddy would not support her in her quest to go to Stanford. He made that clear as he belittled her dream to become a doctor, but she wanted to create a legacy for herself, and nobody was going to stop that. *Now what?* Chelsea's mind kept circling questions over and over. The only clear thing was that Chelsea was going to keep the baby. But how would she even care for a baby? How was she going to move away and go to Stanford with a child?

BACK AT SCHOOL, JESSICA met Chelsea at her locker after school.

"Let's go to my car to talk," Chelsea whispered.

"Okay," Jessica said before noting Chelsea's distressed look. "Wait, are you okay?" Jessica said with her arm around her as they walked to the car. Jessica could tell Chelsea had been crying.

Once they were in the car, Chelsea pulled out the pink slip of paper and handed it to Jessica. Jessica took a moment to read it and then shook her head. She pulled Chelsea into a tight embrace and said, "I'm so sorry. I'm so sorry, Chels. Are you going to tell Freddy?"

Chelsea stared ahead, hardly blinking, like a deer in headlights.

"Yes. I called Freddy. We're meeting after this to talk," Chelsea replied. After a moment, she continued. "Later tonight, I'll tell my mom."

Chelsea bit her lip as she scanned her classmates, breaking up into groups, and getting into cars. Everyone was leaving school and looked so carefree while she felt trapped. "I don't know what to do, Jess. I'm so scared." Chelsea began to cry again as she looked over to see Jessica getting tears in her eyes, too. "I can't believe I'm pregnant. I keep waiting to wake up from a dream. I know nothing about how to care for a baby. Hell, I'm not even seventeen yet! I'm just . . . I'm so confused, I guess," she sobbed, burying her head in her hands.

"I love you, and it will be okay. You are the most caring person I know, and you will be the best mom," Jessica soothed.

After a short while, Chelsea pulled out of the hug. "I probably need to go."

Jessica nodded. "Go talk to Freddy, and I'll call you later."

Chelsea sighed, dried her eyes, and said, "Freddy should be at the park already."

They hugged once more before Jessica hopped out of the car. Chelsea started the car as she watched Jessica walk back into the school.

"Here we go," she mumbled out loud with a deep breath before pulling out of the parking lot.

She drove to the park, the same park where the baby growing inside her had been conceived, and soon she saw Freddy. She pulled into a parking space next to where Freddy was leaning against a tree.

She rolled down the window. "Get in."

Freddy climbed into the passenger seat and tried to hug her. She stuck her hand out to stop him and pulled the pink paper out from under the seat. She let out a big sigh. "I'm pregnant. I found out today."

Freddy's eyes widened, and his face turned red. "You can say I raped you, or I'll pay for an abortion. I once heard that if you sit in a hot tub every night for hours, the fetus won't grow."

Chelsea's eyes narrowed, her mouth opened in disgust, and she couldn't help but stare.

"I'm keeping the baby. I would never kill it," she said, appalled, shaking her head and looking away from him. "Not really the response I was expecting, but whatever. Now you know. Please get out."

Freddy started to say something and then stopped. He was taken aback by her reaction, and the following glare indicated he should stay quiet.

"Um," Freddy mumbled, "okay." He promptly jumped out of the car.

Chelsea peeled out of the parking stall and down the road. *He wants me to kill the baby or tell people he raped me? What the hell is he thinking? I'm pregnant, and that is what he tells me. What a prick!* Tears began flowing down her cheeks again.

LATER THAT NIGHT, CHELSEA's mom looked over toward her and asked, "Honey, what is wrong? I can tell you have been crying."

Chelsea swallowed hard, pulled the pink paper out from her pocket, and handed it to her mom.

"Mom, I'm pregnant," she sighed.

Her mom looked at the pink paper. As she read it, her eyes and her mouth were frozen wide open in a stunned expression. She was silent for a moment and then cried, "Oh no! Chels!"

Chelsea said nothing as she tried to hold back more tears.

Her mom set the paper down and hugged her youngest daughter. "Do you want me to tell your dad?"

Chelsea nodded her head and gave a meek, "Yes."

After moments of silence, Chelsea asked, "Can I go stay over at friend's house tonight while you talk to him?"

Her mom nodded, and Chelsea darted away to pack some clothes.

I think I'll head over to Ryder's house. His parents always said if I needed something, I was welcome.

THAT NIGHT, CHELSEA DIDN'T sleep at all. She felt absolutely sick, tired, and nauseated. At about 2 A.M., she walked out of the guest room and into the kitchen to get water. She saw Freddy sitting there, talking to Ryder. She rolled her eyes, grabbed a bottle of water, and headed back into the bedroom. Freddy followed.

"Wait," he pleaded, grabbing her wrist. She flipped around, shaking him off.

"What do you want?" Chelsea hissed, wanting to yell, but not wanting to wake up Ryder's family.

"I am so sorry, Chels. I didn't mean what I said earlier. I was scared, and I didn't want to hurt you. I have always loved you, and I want you to marry me," Freddy sobbed.

Chelsea stood there staring for a minute, watching the grown man cry in front of her, and she felt twinges of sympathy.

She stood there for a minute in silence, *I can't marry him. He is not who I want in my life, but if I don't marry him, what will my parents do?*

Chelsea sighed. "Look, Freddy, I turn seventeen years old next week, and I found out I'm pregnant. I can't think about one more thing, I'm going back to bed." With that, she pushed him out of the room, shut the door, and cried herself to sleep.

Chapter 5
LEAPING INTO ADULTHOOD

WEEKS HAD PASSED SINCE Chelsea announced the news. She started talking to her parents more about her pregnancy and tried to calm them both down about it. Her dad was ready to file charges for statutory rape against Freddy, convinced that "the hoodlum" needed to be locked up for good. However, Chelsea convinced him she was going to marry Freddy and that it was going to be alright.

She wasn't lying, exactly. She did love him, but she also knew he wasn't the man for her. Still, it seemed like marriage was the best thing to do under the circumstances. She didn't want to marry him because she was pregnant, but between the insurance, he could provide through his work, the support they could both give the baby, and the peace of mind, it was the best solution. As she felt the baby growing inside her, she knew it indicated her dreams would have to be put on hold, even if it meant jumping into adulthood faster than she had planned.

She started focusing her energy on other things, like her excitement for the baby and for a happy marriage.

"I'll get married and try to graduate a year early. That way, I can focus on working, my marriage, and the baby without the worry of school," she explained to family and friends.

Word spread around the high school that she was pregnant. She would walk down the halls and hear snickers, whispers, and name-calling, which was hard to ignore.

In addition to her newfound infamy at school, Chelsea found her quickly approaching adulthood to be far more terrifying. She was throwing up every single day, several times a day, as part of her morning sickness that never stuck to just the morning hours. Her pants didn't fit, and she couldn't afford to buy new clothes, so she stopped by the local thrift store for a couple of pairs of elastic pants. Everywhere she went throughout the school, she couldn't help but hear the whispers of people mocking how she was dressed.

She knew it all was temporary, and she was doing the best that she could. She also knew she wouldn't have to see any of the people mocking her in a few months, which helped as she studied day and night to graduate early. She knew if she kept attending early morning classes and evening classes, it would all be over soon. Her will to succeed was as strong as the morning sickness was long.

ONE DAY AT SCHOOL, while in the rest room throwing up, she could hear Hannah's voice. Hannah was a grade-school bully who had followed Chelsea to every school she had attended and never seemed to tire of teasing Chelsea or her friends. Chelsea paid little attention to her, though, because any negative personality was something she rarely welcomed into her life.

"I heard Chelsea had a miscarriage because she isn't even showing. She's making it all up for attention," Hannah snickered with her friends. Chelsea, alone in the stall behind them, rolled her eyes. Hannah continued, "I also heard she was living out on the streets because her parents had kicked her out. Maybe that is why she is wearing haggard clothes."

At this, Chelsea felt like enough was enough. Her parents weren't perfect, but they were supportive of her, and as much as Chelsea could stand insults thrown her way, she'd be damned if she'd let Hannah insult her family.

Chelsea opened the stall, glared at Hannah, and hissed, "I still live at home, thanks." She pulled up her shirt to display the baby bump and rubbed her belly while wiggling her hips, "and I still look better than you." Hannah, infuriated, sputtered as her friends' laughter turned from Chelsea to Hannah. They walked out as Chelsea washed her hands, a smug smirk on her face.

When she got to her locker, the smile on her face dropped. The word "SLUT" had been written on her locker door with a black Sharpie in bold, big letters. She took a good, long stare at the word before she opened her locker, grabbed her books, and headed to her next class. She knew it had to be Hannah, and she knew Hannah would never get in trouble for it, so she shook it off and decided to clean the word off later.

AFTER CLASS, SHE WAS walking back to her locker when she saw her teammates gathered around it. The whole team seemed to be there, cleaning off the despicable word. They noticed her walking toward them and rushed over to her.

Teri looked at Chelsea and insisted, "Don't listen to them."

Chelsea nodded her head and batted the tears from her eyes as she sighed. "I don't have time to spend on childish people. I'm too tired and sick. I need to graduate and get out of here." Her team nodded in agreement, each of them hugging her as the crowd blocked the hall.

Jessica consoled her. "You only have two more months, and then this petty high school shit will be gone forever. You've got this." Chelsea nodded as she leaned into Jessica's hug.

Chelsea walked away, leaving the cleaning up to her friends, and she went straight to the library to get the next day's homework done before night school. On the way, Chelsea was stopped by someone calling her from inside a classroom.

"Chels, come here. I have a surprise for you," Ms. Warren, the school counselor, exclaimed.

Chelsea always felt that Ms. Warren was a fantastic example of love for students. She was Chelsea's biggest cheerleader in the administration and had helped her rearrange her schedule to be able to graduate early. Chelsea walked over to Ms. Warren and saw a lunch bag.

"You brought me dinner? I love you so much. Thank you!" Chelsea gushed while hugging her and scarfing down the food as quickly as she could.

Most of the time, Ms. Warren made Chelsea dinner, which was the only meal she would get after lunch. She left for school at 6 A.M. and didn't return home until around 10 P.M.

After eating, Chelsea walked into the bathroom and prayed the food would stay down. She looked into the mirror with tears rolling down her cheeks and sobbed, *in a world full of horrible people, I'm so glad I have people who still let me believe there is kindness in this world.*

Chapter 6
BITING OFF MORE THAN YOU CAN CHEW

———

CHELSEA WALKED INTO THE house, excited it was Friday and that she could sleep in the next day. But then she remembered she couldn't, in fact, sleep in because she had a doctor's appointment early the following day. *Oh no, I'd better remind Freddy of the appointment in the morning!* She picked up the phone.

Ring! Ring!

"Hello," Freddy slurred.

"Freddy, remember that tomorrow we have that doctor's appointment at 8 A.M. They will tell us the sex of the baby, okay?" Chelsea told him.

"Why are they doing it on a Saturday at 8 A.M.?" Freddy asked, clearly annoyed about Chelsea's late-night call and the early morning appointment on the weekend.

"Look, the doctor isn't even open on Saturdays, but he's doing me a favor and working around my school schedule. You don't have to go, but that's when it is, and I'd appreciate you being there," she sighed.

Chelsea quickly hung up the phone and was instantly annoyed that Freddy was so put out over an early appointment. She went to all of her other baby appointments alone, and he made a big deal about wanting to be invited, only to act like it was a considerable inconvenience. "I am barely sleeping, and I'm working my ass off to graduate. I am planning a wedding. I'm pregnant and sick, and he has the nerve to bitch to me about making an appointment at 8 A.M.," she groaned in disbelief as she was getting ready for bed. "Unbelievable."

CHELSEA SAT IN THE waiting room at Dr. Nelson's office, watching for Freddy. She kept trying to call him, but he didn't answer. After more than fifteen minutes of waiting, she went into Dr. Nelson's office.

"It's okay. We can find out the baby's sex without him. I doubt he's coming," she sighed.

Dr. Nelson was very kind to Chelsea. She appreciated that he never treated her like she was a worthless teen mom, which most seemed to do when they found out she was pregnant.

"This is an ultrasound machine. Let's have you lie down," he said, and he began to apply cold jelly to her stomach. He then placed the device on her belly, and she could immediately hear the thumping of the baby's heartbeat.

It sounds like racehorses running around a track. Chelsea looked at the monitor and could see a little banana-shaped baby.

"Oh, my gosh. It looks like a curled up banana," Chelsea said, laughing.

He asked, "So, are you hoping for a boy or a girl?"

Chelsea laughed and exclaimed, "Definitely a girl. The outfits are cuter."

"Well, guess what? You are in luck because it is a girl!" he replied, smiling at her.

She squealed with excitement, and then a rush of fear overcame her. He saw her demeanor change and asked, "Is something wrong?"

She shook her head and stammered, "It all seems so real now."

The doctor smiled, and they talked about her persistent morning sickness.

"Well, the baby is growing well, even if you can't keep any food down. Babies are like parasites. They take everything from your body," Dr. Nelson said with a grin.

He walked out of the room and came back in with a girl's newborn blanket to congratulate her. It was pink with little elephants on it and had a built-in hood for the head.

"Aw. It is adorable," she gushed, holding it close. "This is the first thing I have ever received for her. Oh, my heavens! For HER!" Chelsea beamed with enthusiasm and a squeak in her voice as she thanked him.

When she went home, she called all of her friends to tell them the news.

She hung the picture of the small looking banana on the fridge so she could see it every time she went into the kitchen.

"It is her first photo," Chelsea said proudly when her parents and sister came to see it.

Freddy finally called her back. "Sorry, babe. I was out drinking last night and missed my alarm." She sighed and hung up the phone on him. She was supposed to see him later that night with Ryder and had every intention to give him a piece of her mind.

She looked at the photo again, *Ah. In two weeks, I'm going to be graduated, married, and over halfway done being pregnant.* The thought of not being sick every second of every day seemed like a dream come true, and the idea of one more saltine cracker made her want to gag.

"Chelsea, call me back," said Freddy on the answering machine. Chelsea was still upset with him for missing the baby's reveal appointment and picked up the phone to give him a piece of her mind. As she lifted up the receiver to dial, her bedroom door opened. It was Freddy.

"What do you want, Freddy? Can't you even make it to one appointment? You can't even show up for her or me?" Chelsea hissed.

"Chels, you're right, I love you, and I promise I will change for you both. I've never wanted anything more in this world than the both of you. I am sorry. I'm so very sorry," Freddy said while he grabbed her hands.

"Her?" he asked after a pause.

"Yes, the baby is a girl," Chelsea said, her voice revealing a calm she didn't actually feel.

After talking for what seemed like hours with Freddy, he said, "Hey, Ryder and his family want us to come over for dinner.

Maybe before that, we can stop by a ring shop and get you a ring that will fit perfectly on that tiny finger of yours." Freddy touched her cheeks and then her belly. "Go and get ready, and let's get you out of here. It's been a while, and I think you need to be pampered."

Chelsea went to get ready, but when she went to her closet, all she could do was let out a sigh. Nothing fit, and it was beyond her comprehension how she could gain any weight at all when she threw up everything that touched her stomach.

She looked at Freddy and said, "I have nothing that fits me. Let me go see if my sister has something."

Sadie had more curves than Chelsea, which meant maybe something would at least fit her expanding hips. After a few minutes of digging around in Sadie's closet, she found a pair of pants and left a note.

I borrowed some pants. I'll wash and return them later — Chels

Ring shopping felt odd to Chelsea because she was already pregnant, a wedding date was already set, and there wasn't really a marriage proposal. The romance of the situation wasn't there, and she felt more like they should be shoe shopping for a good pair of heels or pants that would fit her.

She found a beautiful, unique marquee diamond she felt suited her and their budget. She told Freddy, and they bought the ring. They purchased it a ring size larger, knowing Chelsea was outgrowing everything.

Freddy smiled at her. "Well, we can afford a little bit bigger diamond if you want."

Chelsea smiled back. "There are more important things to buy than a ring, and I don't need anything flashy. I like the simple and unique design. It is perfect."

They walked out of the store, and she kept feeling the ring on her hand. It was odd to have something on her ring finger. *That ring is two months' rent. Speaking of rent, where are we going to live?* Chelsea stopped walking and said, "Babe? Where are we going to live?"

Freddy looked at her and said, "Well, my parents are building their basement, and I'm going to help them finish it. We will pay rent, and then they will give us back all of the rent after ten months so we can buy a home with it. Plus, remember we will get government assistance for food for you and the baby."

"Government assistance? Isn't that for poor people?" Chelsea asked and then remembered she was as poor as they came. Her parents were paying the thousand dollars for their wedding to help. Next to that, she had nothing monetarily speaking, and she couldn't work until she finished school.

Freddy looked at her, smiled, and reassured her. "It will be okay," he said, before distracting her with baby items.

For dinner, they stopped by Ryder's house. As they were all sitting around, enjoying the quiet stillness, when out of the blue, Ryder looked at Freddy and said, "Either you tell her, or I will. I swear to God, Freddy, she is the perfect girl and deserves to know."

Freddy shot Ryder a look. Chelsea looked at them both. "What the hell is up with you two? You two have acted oddly all night."

Freddy started to stutter, grabbed Chelsea, and said, "Um, Chels, umm, well, you know when the baby was conceived?"

Chelsea looked at him, incredulously. "Well, yes. It was the second time I ever had sex. Of course, I know when the baby was conceived, Why?" Her eyebrows were furrowed, and she wished he would hurry and get to the point.

"Chels, I love you more than anything or anyone on this earth." He paused and then continued. "When you broke up with me after New Year's Day, I couldn't imagine losing the best thing that has ever happened to me. You make me happy."

"Get to the point, Freddy," Chelsea said after he paused to look at Ryder again. He looked like a guilty child talking to an angry parent, hoping he wouldn't have to apologize.

Freddy continued. "Um. Well, it is just that I feel whole when you are around. When I saw you with that Travis guy, it killed me to think of you with someone else."

Freddy's hands were shaking, and he was visibly sweating. Ryder was looking over, giving him a daring look to continue.

"Well, you see, Chels, I invited you to that party, and then I took you on that truck ride so I could have sex with you again."

Chelsea interrupted. "Well, no duh. So what? You didn't know I would get pregnant."

Freddy's eyebrow raised. Ryder's mouth opened to speak, and then he quickly shut it.

"What the hell? You knew I would get pregnant? How? That makes no sense. We used protection," Chelsea said, shaking her head.

Freddy explained, "Baby, I am so sorry. I didn't completely think about what all of this would do to your life. What it would do to both of our lives. What it would do to us. I put a hole in the condom because I didn't want you to leave me." He moved over and grabbed her. "I didn't want to lose you. I couldn't bear to lose you. I got you pregnant on purpose, and I am so sorry."

Chelsea immediately felt a flush of heat flow through her body. She darted for the bathroom to throw up.

After forty-five minutes of throwing up and crying, she walked out and shouted, "I think I need to go home. Can you please take me home?"

On the ride, every time Freddy would try to talk, she would look over and say, "Can you please give me time and silence?" and Freddy would immediately stop with what he was trying to say.

They pulled into the driveway of Chelsea's house. Chelsea spoke slowly and with purpose. "I understand that you didn't want to lose me and also your fear of abandonment. I get my part in all of this as well. It takes two to tango."

Chelsea paused, took a deep breath, and continued. "I'm committed to making our marriage work. I'm committed to this little baby girl. I expect the same commitment on your part, mainly since you actively asked for this. I am so disappointed in you. I need space to clear my head. Please be respectful of that."

Chelsea hopped out of the car, and Freddy sat in the vehicle as she entered the house.

"He purposely got me pregnant. Did he put a hole in the condom to trap me to stay with him? I was only sixteen years old, and he wanted to trap me?" Chelsea sobbed.

Chapter 7
BUTTERFLY FLUTTERS

S CHELSEA WALKED THROUGH a garden of plumerias, she saw children playing in the yard. They were spinning round and round on a merry-go-round, screaming with glee. Next to them, she saw a small baby in a carriage. She smiled and started to walk over to join them.

As she was walking, she saw a wolf and its cubs eating their prey with their steel gray claws extended into the victim. The wolf's close-set golden eyes had a penetrating stare on the children. Chelsea sprinted toward the children as she saw the wolf's teeth showing through its long, cringed snout. She knew the wolf was ready to attack the children, and she needed to help them.

The wolf saw her and started to run after her with her fangs out, snapping with each step. "God, please protect us all," she screamed as she grabbed the baby, tucked it in close to her, and curled into the tightest ball she could as the wolf pounced on her.

Beep! Beep! Beep! The alarm went off. She woke up sweating and visibly shaking.

Today was her wedding day. That dream was undoubtedly not the kind of dream she wanted to have going into one of the biggest days of her life.

She stared at the ceiling, trying to calm herself down. *I wonder what that dream meant? Maybe it was because I missed my graduation yesterday? It was just a piece of paper, but it was a hard few months for that piece of paper.*

Still, she felt satisfaction for graduating early. Although Chelsea didn't get a graduation party, she was excited to be done and going out of town for a couple days for her honeymoon.

"In four more months, I will have my adorable baby girl. She will be worth all I have sacrificed to prepare for her," she declared to herself as she was getting out of bed.

She stretched, feeling her belly and the baby's kicks. They felt like little butterfly flutters in her stomach. Chelsea had always heard that one day, pregnant people pop, and pop was right. Her belly seemed twice the size it had been the day before.

"Oh, goodness! I guess I really am pregnant after all," she muttered to herself as she headed to the bathroom.

Soon, Jessica arrived to help Chelsea get ready.

As Chelsea and Jessica were in the bathroom jibber-jabbering, the rest of the girls came in to join them. Jessica zipped up the back of Chelsea's dress and declared, "Oh, wow. It fits like a glove."

Chelsea laughed. "I popped overnight. It is insane. I look like I have half a soccer ball in my belly. I guess I really am pregnant and not getting fat."

She gave them a wink and asked, "Y'all, ready for this?"

Jessica looked over and replied, "Are *you* ready for this?"

One thing Chelsea loved about Jessica was that she always expressed her concern for her friend first. She would put it all out on the table and then support whatever decisions Chelsea made, including the ones that she didn't agree with, and this happened to be one of those.

She looked over as the bridesmaids started getting dressed and smiled. Then she grabbed the hairspray and sprayed her hair a dozen more times, knowing it might melt in the sun. It was a hot May day, but the flowers were in full bloom, and the sun glistened. The backyard looked like a catalog photo, and she knew how many hours her family spent making it look so pristine. The day was perfect, and Chelsea felt good.

Jessica walked over and put a flower in her hair and said, "You are beautiful! Your mom says they are ready. Let's go." Chelsea smiled, let out a sigh, and stared out into the living room. The plan was to walk from the deck, down the deck stairs, and to the archway.

Chelsea's aunt was a fantastic singer. She sang while the bridesmaids and flower girls were walking down the aisle. She then belted out the traditional "Here Comes the Bride," and Chelsea started to walk out.

She walked onto the deck, and everyone stood, smiling at her as she made her way down the stairs. *Oh, God! Please don't let me trip and fall.* She watched as she walked in heels down the path they had made. Heels had never been a problem before the big bump in her midsection, but now that she could barely see her feet, they were becoming a hindrance.

She looked around and saw the sunshine beaming down on her. The archway filled with flowers and the pristine yard. She heard the trickling water of the fountains, birds chirping and awes from the audience. She took it all in as she handed her bouquet to Jessica, and she turned to look at Freddy. He grabbed her hand and held it while the priest performed the ceremony.

Oh, my God! I feel like I need to run away now, as she then took a deep breath. This was not what she wanted in life, but she had made a commitment. *I need to be grateful for all I have. I have a lot more than most.*

Before she knew it, she heard the fateful words, "I now pronounce you husband and wife. You may kiss the bride."

Freddy kissed her sloppily, then hugged her and whispered, "We did it!"

At that moment she heard a crash and then a gasp from someone in the audience. She looked over to see that the cake had toppled over. It melted right off the table. The ornament on top was shattered in a million pieces all over the ground.

Chelsea walked over to it, smiled, and chuckled. "I hope nobody wanted cake."

Chapter 8
EVER-CHANGING INSANITY

CHELSEA WAS PACING THE floor as she continued to look out the window every five minutes. "Oh, my hell, where is he?" she kept saying as she sat with her herbal tea, holding the four-week-old baby, Tabatha, close to her chest.

She needed to leave for work in fifteen minutes, and Freddy was nowhere to be found. She walked upstairs to find her in-laws. As they heard the door open, they instantly woke up.

Chelsea said softly, "I am so sorry to wake you, but Freddy never came home last night, and I have to go to work. I cannot afford to miss work, and I don't know what else to do with Tabby. I'm sure he will be home soon."

Sharla, Freddy's stepmom, opened her arms. She seemed thrilled to have a baby in the house. She walked into the living room where the rocker was, and Chelsea went downstairs to get the baby's bag.

When she came back upstairs, she sat down next to her and said, "Sharla, can I ask you something?"

Sharla smiled and said, "Of course you can."

Chelsea smiled back and took a deep breath. Sharla looked so happy, Chelsea didn't want to bring her down. "Never mind. It's too early for all of this, and I have to go. I'll talk to you later."

Sharla spoke up. "I will watch her anytime. I also know that if he comes home drunk, I will not let him near her, and I will have his dad set that boundary."

Chelsea laughed. "Clearly, you knew what I was going to ask. Thank you for being so understanding, and I'm so sorry to impose. I know you have young children of your own."

Chelsea paused and then continued, "I'm anxious when he is around her. He told me he felt like shaking her when she cried. I'm so worried now whenever I leave him with her. His temper is awful and scary." Chelsea stopped and hugged them both. "Thank you again, and I love you."

Sharla knew all about Freddy's temper, and his parents knew to keep a close eye out for their son.

It still blew Chelsea's mind that she had married this man—a man who purposely wanted her pregnant, an ex-drug user, a vast partier, and someone who had contemplated murder.

As she was pulling out of the driveway, a car pulled recklessly into the driveway, almost hitting her. It was Freddy. He jumped out of the vehicle and stumbled and staggered over to her car, his lip bulging with chewing tobacco.

"Aren't you going to give me a kiss, goodbye?" he asked.

Chelsea looked at him, disgusted. "You know damn well, my job requires me to open the building and the phone lines at a certain time. You have a baby and a wife." Chelsea paused as she felt her blood boiling. "You barely got your license back, and now you are driving drunk? It's time to grow up and act like an adult. You'd better be going to work. I don't care that you spent all night drinking and partying. Get your act together!"

She put the car in reverse and peeled out of the driveway.

"He is the worst human on the planet!" she spat out loud to herself. "I hope he gets the night job. Then I don't have to see him most days. I'm starting to hate him."

"Chelsea, you're late!" Karen, the manager, stated.

"Karen, I know, I am so sorry. I tried to get out in time, but the baby...Never mind. I'll make sure it doesn't happen again," Chelsea explained.

Karen was a heavyset woman with white hair that resembled a mop. She seemed to be on a constant power trip as she would dish out passive-aggressive insults to Chelsea. Karen made it clear she wouldn't have hired Chelsea if she knew she was a pregnant teen who had to get married.

I wonder if all bosses are like her or if I'm just lucky enough to get a job with one.

She loved the job itself. She would take messages for people who needed to see a professional, ranging from doctors, dentists, vets, and accountants. The customers loved her, and she was positive that Karen despised that part the most. Chelsea was the fastest, friendliest, and most reliable employee she had, and that seemed to make Karen's blood boil with rage daily.

"One day, when I have employees, I'm going to value them and respect them," she muttered under her breath to herself.

Chapter 9
HOMEOWNERSHIP

⁓

*I*T WAS MOVING DAY! Chelsea worked six extra months to meet the requirements of the mortgage lenders to qualify and purchase her own home.

It was one of the cheapest homes on the market, but while all of her friends were excited about their senior trips, she was grateful she had a home to call her very own. She didn't care that a dishwasher was now her idea of excitement. It was a luxury when she had so little. Chelsea had been working two jobs for months to earn enough money to put down on a home because Freddy's parents reneged on their original agreement to give the couple back what they paid in rent.

"Now, the goal is to have only one job with better pay," she said to herself, looking in the mirror of the moving truck. "My situation won't be forever. Sure, things seem to keep going wrong, but one day they have to go right."

Chelsea looked back and thought about how much she had been working. She had gone eighteen months with only three consecutive days off of work. She was up at 4 A.M. and in bed around 11 P.M.

I sure hope Freddy will get a stable income soon. He misses so many days at work, and he is always out late. But I'd rather have my husband partying at a bar than in my and Tabby's space.

Tabby loved sleeping in Chelsea's bed with her. The two of them spent any free time Chelsea had together. She was a temperamental child but was always happy if cartoons were on, so television shows were on as much as Chelsea could tolerate.

Her friends and family showed up to help their family move. Even Freddy's biological mom showed up to help. They didn't have much at all, but they had enough to buy a small rambler with three bedrooms, a bathroom, and a kitchen.

This is all we need.

Chelsea scrambled to get the right keys and opened the door. She peered inside, and her stomach dropped. "Oh my God, this is horrible," she gasped.

Her family and friends walked through the trashed home. The walls were yellow and brown, the toilets were black, there were gobs of hair in the sink, and the bathtub was the grossest thing Chelsea had ever seen.

"When we looked at the home, it was dark, the windows were closed, and people were still in it," Chelsea explained to the family as she noticed the looks of mortification on their faces.

This was absolutely the most disgusting house Chelsea had ever been in, and now it was hers. *No wonder it was the cheapest one on the market and took a while to sell. But it has three bed-rooms. It just needs lots of cleaning.*

Chelsea's mom looked at her, touched her hand, and said, "Well, let me run to the store to get some cleaning supplies before we start moving stuff in here."

Chelsea looked at her and said, "Thanks, mom!"

It didn't matter what Chelsea needed, she could always rely on her mom and Sadie to help. They also spoiled Tabby, and Chelsea was forever thankful for the endless supply of clothing for her. Her family really did rally around Chelsea and tried to support her in any way they could. Both of her parents still worked, and her sister worked, but if she was ever in a pinch, she could rely on them for anything she asked.

Her family knew she was struggling to have Freddy watch Tabby. One time, he almost yanked Tabby's arm out of the socket because she was fussy. He swung the small six-month-old baby by the arm to pick her up, upset her binky wasn't working.

After that incident, her family no longer tried to convince or question Chelsea on why she didn't want to leave the baby with Freddy.

"CHELSEA, WE HAVE TO go home. It has been eight hours of washing walls. I'm sorry we can't help move stuff to where it goes," her mother said.

There were sighs of agreement from the rest of her friends and family, and it made sense.

"Thank you for coming. It means the world to us. Let's put everything in the middle of the living room, and we can move it later," Chelsea said.

She continued to clean throughout the night, knowing that she only had two days until she returned to work, and she had to have the home in order. Chelsea loved being a mom to Tabby, but nights like those, she felt isolated and alone. She understood that she wasn't like other seventeen-year-olds, and it was her path, but it felt like more than she could bear too.

Chelsea looked in the mirror and wiped her tears away and exclaimed, "I need a bath so bad, but I can't get in that tub until I soak off the black in it."

As she was scrubbing the tub, water got on her skin. "Oh, my God! Is the water acid?" she yelped as she ripped off the gloves and examined her hands and forearms to see that the bleach had eaten away at her skin, even with gloves on.

I need to keep cleaning and get it over the pain, but the water on my arms is torture.

"Snap out of it, Chelsea. Get out of "poor me" mode, and get to work," she said out loud to herself. She walked into the other room and put on some music and then set up the baby swing for Tabby and placed her in it.

"I love you, baby! Mommy is cleaning and can't bear for you to touch a thing," Chelsea said as she kissed her and went back to cleaning.

"Soon, you are going to quit your two jobs and work for the government. You will work there like your family members, and you will have this home to fix up. It is perfect for us," she asserted, trying to motivate herself to keep moving. Right, when she felt like she couldn't move any longer, her door opened, and there was Jessica.

"Alrighty, let's get this party started!" Jessica joked.

It was like Jessica to know Chelsea was in desperate need of her help. *I swear, anytime I'm ready to have a breakdown, Jessica pops on over.* Chelsea removed her gloves and gave her a big hug.

"Now, let's get to work," Jessica said as she grabbed Tabby out of her swing and began feeding her and dressing her into her pajamas. "Okay, sweetie, you are ready for bed."

She put Tabby back into her swing to fall asleep.

She then turned to Chelsea and said, "Hey, let's get started on your room so you can sleep."

Jessica grabbed the boombox and moved it into Chelsea's room. She then sprinted out to her car and walked back in with their favorite playlist. "Guess what I brought?" Jessica chirped.

"Um, let me guess—eighties music," Chelsea said, laughing as she grabbed the CD. "You are the best ever."

I guess I'm not as isolated and alone as I was whining about.

After a couple of hours, Jessica declared, "Okay! Chels, your bedroom is put together. You sleep, and I'll come back tomorrow."

Chelsea smiled at her as she walked with her to the front door. "I appreciate you more than you'll ever know."

She walked to the swing where Tabby was sound asleep. She picked her up and placed her onto her bed. "I'll see you in a few hours. I love you," she whispered.

She picked up the boombox and carried it out of the room and into the bathroom.

I will not be sleeping tonight. I can't sleep when I know this house is not even sanitary enough for Tabby to roam around in. At least Freddy is working. I certainly cannot handle his drunk ass today.

Chapter 10
WORK-LIFE BALANCE

ABOUT A MONTH AND a half into the position, Burt, the manager of the tire store, came up to Chelsea's desk.

Burt was a rather bulky and extremely tall man who had to duck as he walked through the doorways. Each day he would walk into the shop, scanning the premises with his grey eyes settling on nothing before he went into his office and closed the door.

Chelsea smiled and asked, "What's up?"

Burt scratched his three-day stubble and said, "Chelsea, we need to do the quarterly books and reports, if you can stay later."

"Of course, I'll get a babysitter. I am excited to learn to file them," Chelsea exclaimed enthusiastically, knowing that staying late would be overtime pay.

Chelsea was on an annual leave known as furlough from her government job and missed the money, but she was grateful Burt offered her the job, even knowing she would leave in a couple months.

I wish I could stay at home like everyone else who is furloughed. Unfortunately, that is not an option since Freddy is skipping work, and I am the bread-winner.

AT CLOSING, BURT WAS showing Chelsea how to do the books, and she was a natural. She continued to finish them while he left to close up the shop and lock the doors.

"Chelsea, can you come down here, please?" asked Burt.

"Yep! On my way," Chelsea said as she started walking down the stairs from the upstairs office.

Burt started walking up the stairs as Chelsea was stepping down.

"What's up?" she asked.

He grabbed her face and tried to kiss her. She shuddered and quickly turned away, which made him miss her mouth and kiss the side of her head.

"What the hell was that?" Chelsea snapped. "I am married, and so are you!"

"Oh, come on, Chels. You know I've had a thing for you, and you have to have a thing for me. Everyone has a thing for me," Burt declared.

Chelsea walked back upstairs, grabbed her lunch pail, and stated, "Don't flatter yourself. Not everyone has a thing for you. I certainly don't, and I'm leaving!"

Burt demanded, "If you leave now, you can kiss your job, goodbye."

Chelsea walked right past him and out the door.

"Oh my hell! A thing for you? A fat, over-aged shop manager? Oh, baby! Not!" she yelled, shaking her head.

She went home and saw Freddy sitting on the couch watching TV with chewing tobacco in his lip, spitting it into a cup. Each time he reached for the container to spit into, she could see a fresh wound on his arm from cutting himself.

What the hell! I'm going to have a nervous breakdown soon. I feel so sick.

"Freddy, can you feed Tabby, please? I'm not feeling terrific and want to take a bath," Chelsea asked in a pleading voice.

Freddy sighed at the inconvenience. "I guess. You do look white like you don't feel well."

Chelsea walked off, *Oh, I'm so glad that I look like shit so you can watch your own child after she's been at a babysitter all day.*

Chelsea ran the bathwater and looked in the mirror as tears rolled down her face. *It would be so lovely if I could confide in my husband about what happened at work, but instead, watching him chew tobacco and cut himself is as close as our relationship gets.*

"Well, I guess I know why Burt hired me for the job," she muttered to herself. "He says everyone has a thing for him. Eww! I can't stand Freddy, but I would never cheat on him either."

THE NEXT DAY, SHE decided to go look for a new job. She stopped by a cleaning company to ask if they were hiring, and they said they were.

She immediately filled out an application and was given the job on the spot. She felt a twinge of guilt because she didn't tell the company about her returning back to her government job in less than two months. She couldn't risk it with the baby, the car, and a mortgage.

Chapter 11
ABIDE AND SEEK

———

*I*T WAS TIME FOR Chelsea to return to her government position. She had been accepted into a new department, criminal investigation, which would allow her to work full-time and year-round, and the pay was higher. It was a department that was sought out by hundreds, but she got it.

Freddy and Chelsea decided to move closer to her job and to his parents. They found a house up the street from her work, and the payments were about the same as they were paying currently. The payments were able to be the same because of all of the sweat equity in fixing it up. It made them fifteen thousand dollars in nine short months.

Freddy was working graveyards, and Chelsea was working days.

"I THINK NOT SEEING him is saving our marriage," she told Jessica one day. "I am so miserable and unhappy. I feel like I am the only one trying for the family—financially, emotionally, physically, and mentally. I am so much younger than Freddy, but I feel like I am his mom instead of his wife. I hate every minute of being married to him."

Jessica agreed with her.

"He looks at Tabby as a huge inconvenience. He looks at me as a huge inconvenience. I don't even care if he leaves us most weekends to party. I'd rather have him gone than have to deal with his negativity and anger."

She reminisced about a time when she was happy. She felt so alone, so empty, and she had so much responsibility at such a young age. Even when she was talking with family and friends, she still felt alone. She was only nineteen years old and wasn't old enough to legally rent a car, go to a bar, or drink alcohol, yet there she was with a baby, home, mortgage, and a job, all of the things adults have.

Quite often, Freddy would come staggering in at night, and Chelsea would pretend to be asleep because if he knew she was awake, he would want to have sex or start a fight about something, and she didn't want to deal with any of it. She felt like her wifely duty of having sex once a week was plenty for her.

ABOUT A WEEK INTO her new job, she walked into the break room, and the smell of tuna fish made her run to the bathroom and throw up. "I must have the flu," she told a concerned coworker.

After a week of being sick, she went to the doctor. One of the perks of working for the government was that she had medical insurance and could finally go to the doctor when she was sick.

The doctor weighed her, and she had lost weight from when she had visited a couple months prior and was prescribed antibiotics for a sinus infection.

"I likely lost weight from stress. I'm struggling in my marriage, and I recently moved and changed jobs," she explained to him.

The doctor looked at her and asked, "Well, that is possible, but is there any way you could be pregnant?"

Chelsea laughed. "Well, I'm on that super-strong birth control pill, and my husband barely touches me, so likely no. It would be almost impossible. I have never, ever missed a pill, and I take them at the same time every single day."

The doctor nodded and smiled. "I see. Well, let's run a blood pregnancy test to confirm."

The doctor drew her blood and gave Tabby a sucker for sitting on the chair so well. He then left to go run the tests.

Why is it taking forever? They realize I have a toddler running around in here—right?

After what seemed like forever, the doctor came back into the room. "It looks like there will be two of her," he said, pointing to Tabby.

Chelsea sat in shock for a moment before asking if Tabby could go to the waiting room to be with the nurse.

As soon as the door shut, she exploded. "What?! Two of her? I'm pregnant?! How? Why?"

She broke into tears.

"Are you sure? I don't get it. I take the pill every single day at the same time. I rarely have sex, and my marriage can't take this," she said sobbing.

The doctor touched her shoulder. "Did you happen to take other precautions when you were sick and on antibiotics?"

Chelsea shook her head in confusion. "What do you mean? No. Why?"

The doctor leaned back, and with compassion, said, "Well, the nurse should have told you that antibiotics reduce the effectiveness of birth control."

Chelsea burst into tears again and shook her head.

"We can talk about options if you like," he suggested when she looked like she was calming down.

Chelsea shook her head. "I'll schedule a follow-up appointment. I guess I'm having another baby before I turn twenty years old."

FOR THE NEXT TWO weeks straight, Chelsea cried herself to sleep. Freddy didn't even notice that something was wrong with her, and to tell him meant she had to deal with him being excited for another baby. He had been begging for another one, but she saw what he was like with the one they already had, so the thought of adding one more seemed too much to bear. *It is puzzling to me why he wants another baby when he doesn't even take care of the child he has,* she thought with anger about Freddy getting his own way, and she knew it would be up to her to take care of another child.

FINALLY, AFTER ALMOST THREE weeks of crying herself to sleep, she told her family and Freddy she was pregnant. She had accepted it and was even starting to get excited about the idea of another baby. She was already a few months pregnant by the time she had found out. She never expected she would get pregnant again so soon, but it had happened, and it was time to get ready.

Chapter 12
OVERLOOKING LIFE LESSONS

———

As the weeks passed, Chelsea watched as her body began to change, then slowly, she noticed a small pudge in her tummy. Like last time, she had wondered if she was actually pregnant until that little pudge appeared.

She began falling in love with the baby growing inside of her, and every morning, she woke up with a smile on her face.

Moreover, everyone seemed thrilled for her. Despite Chelsea's age, she didn't seem to have as many judging eyes on her this time around. She also wasn't as sick, and she was eternally thankful for that.

She went to her doctor's appointments like clockwork and left each appointment relieved and thrilled to discover that everything was exactly how it should be. She first heard the baby's heartbeat in the doctor's office a month after finding out, and she cried tears of joy. She wanted to find out the sex, but the baby was modest, and the doctor couldn't tell during the ultrasound, so she figured she'd wait until the next month.

She had begun preparing for the baby by cleaning everything, decorating the room, and shopping—all the things she didn't have time for when she was pregnant with Tabby. A two-seated stroller had caught her eye, and she decided that maybe she should start saving up. She could get exercise by continuing to run in the morning with her two little ones. She enjoyed imagining all three of them getting out in the fresh air.

ONE NIGHT AS SHE was getting Tabby into the bathtub, she felt a burst of pain in her stomach. She chalked it up to growing pains because her belly was definitely increasing, but the pain didn't stop, so she decided she would take a bath once Tabby was tucked into bed. The pain seemed to get worse as the night went on.

When Chelsea climbed into the tub later that night, she noticed she had lost a lot of blood. She panicked and ran to the bedroom, soaking wet. She picked up the phone to call her doctor, only to discover he was unavailable, and she was transferred to the doctor who was on call.

The on-call doctor asked for her symptoms. After describing the pain and hearing that she had lost a lot of blood, he said callously, "Well, it sounds like you're having a miscarriage. Unless you are lying in a puddle of blood, there is nothing we can do about that. Go to the ER if you start bleeding heavily." And he hung up.

AFTER AN HOUR, CHELSEA broke down crying as she called out to Freddy, "I'm in labor now." She began throwing on a dress and flip-flops. "We have to go to the ER now."

There was no way that having contractions like these could be normal. Can you even have contractions during a miscarriage? Who knows? All she knew was that she needed to get to the hospital ASAP.

Chelsea's contractions were three minutes apart by the time Freddy made it out to the car. She had called a neighbor to watch Tabby, and as they headed for the hospital, she saw their neighbor, a nice, elderly woman, rushing toward their door and into the house with a quick wave as they took off down the road.

THE ER NURSES WERE supportive and helpful and tried to get the monitors strapped on properly to check for the baby's heartbeat.

"Chelsea is fully dilated. Let's get her into another room," the doctor announced to the nurse after checking her in. A look of concern crept across the hospital staff's faces.

Before Chelsea knew what was happening, she saw her environment turn quiet with looks of panic and whispering. She started crying and praying, not knowing what was happening, but she knew that in her heart, she was losing the baby.

I'm far enough along, but I didn't hear the heartbeat when they put on the monitors.

The doctor left the room and talked to the nurses. She sat there, watching them through the hospital's glass door to her room and could feel significant pain and sadness as she saw their frowns.

The doctor walked back into the room a short minute later. "I'm sorry, but the baby is no longer alive, and you are losing massive amounts of blood. We need to do a DNC now," he told her as a nurse prepped a syringe. "We are going to administer pain medication now and put you to sleep."

They placed her on another gurney and wheeled her into the surgical hall. She looked over and saw Freddy standing in the corner, crying next to another doctor she had met earlier. She felt her eyes getting heavy, and everything seemed foggy, but she wasn't feeling any more pain. Then she drifted off into sleep.

THERE WAS THAT FAMILIAR waterfall, the lush trees, and the plumerias all around. Chelsea could hear the sound of the water and could smell the fragrances. She felt the sun beating down and warming her.

She heard laughter and began to walk through the field toward the sound. It was children's laughter. She saw a group of people from a distance. They looked over and smiled at her. She couldn't see who they were, but she knew that she knew them somehow. She began walking and could see the sun shining on one spot in particular. She asked, "Is that God?"

She wanted to go find out. She started walking faster. Then running. Yet they seemed to get further and further away until the light turned into a flashlight shining in her eyes. It was the doctor saying over and over, "Chelsea, Chelsea."

She opened her eyes and closed them again. She wanted to return to the field but kept hearing, "Chelsea, you need to wake up now and take deep breaths."

She willed herself to breathe. She felt so weak and tired, and she wanted to go to sleep again.

"Chelsea, do you think you can breathe deeply for us and sit up?" She started to sit up and saw the nurses, the doctor, and Freddy.

Freddy rushed to her with swollen eyes, as the doctor began doing checks as she was regaining consciousness. "Chelsea, we had to take the baby. There was nothing you did wrong or could have done to prevent it."

The doctor paused, took a breath and continued, "Your surgery was an emergency surgery, and there is a lot of scar tissue, so we need to see you in a couple weeks to discuss the possibility of a hysterectomy."

Chelsea blinked. "You mean, I can't have any more kids?"

The doctor looked down briefly, then continued. "The chances are slim due to the damage your body endured, but let's talk in a couple weeks. I would also like you to start to think about filing a complaint about the doctor on call. What you were told, without him knowing how far along you were, was malpractice, and I am sorry. The baby was likely already gone, but the complications of the labor could have been prevented. Let's talk in a couple of weeks."

THE NEXT DAY, CHELSEA was released from the hospital. She was already sporting a large bruise on her hand from the IV.

It was so weird, being pregnant one day and then not the next. Then being told that Tabby was going to be an only child. Chelsea didn't know how to feel yet.

She kept thinking back to her dream, where she heard the laughter from multiple children. It felt so real.

Freddy kept trying to talk to her about things she didn't understand. She stopped him. "I'm confused, tired, and in a daze. Let's talk later."

She thought the miscarriage was her fault for being unappreciative of the gift when she first heard she was pregnant. Now she might never have another child, and the thought was killing her.

Chapter 13
EXPECT THE UNEXPECTED

THREE WEEKS AFTER TRYING, she felt like she might be pregnant again. She told her family, and they all assumed she had lost her mind, but somehow, she felt like she was pregnant. She waited for another two weeks and went to the doctor. The doctor began the consultation with a sad statement. "Sometimes we wish for something so much, even though it cannot happen. Have you had a period this month?"

Chelsea said, "Nope. I'm a week past, but I can't wait any longer, so I have to know."

The doctor smiled pitifully. "Well, let's do a test and see. Did you happen to file those legal documents on the malpractice?"

Chelsea looked at him as she shook her head and explained, "You know, that mistake will ruin that doctor's career. I already have a beautiful daughter, and I don't feel like it's the right thing to do to someone. He didn't know how far along I was, and I figured I would wait and see what the upcoming month says about my health and fertility before I file charges and damage a career that took decades to build."

The doctor looked at her with admiration and touched her arm. "You know, for such a young woman, you sure are wise and forgiving. I'll send the nurse in to draw some blood unless you would like an ultrasound now instead. It should be covered by your insurance due to recent trauma."

Chelsea smiled and said, "Definitely the ultrasound."

The doctor asked her to lie down and put some ice-cold jelly on her already flat tummy. He gently pressed the device onto her stomach. She immediately heard what sounded like a horse galloping. She grinned. "I know what that means."

The doctor looked at the screen with amazement. "These are the times when I love to say I was wrong," he said, as the two of them watched the grey screen before them. "Congratulations! Let's get you scheduled for your next appointment. And let's treat this as a high-risk pregnancy, so take it easy, okay?"

Chelsea nodded and hurried home so she could tell her mom, sister, and dad. She would wait to tell Freddy when he came back from work.

She looked at the calendar to put in her next appointment and realized that today was also the due date of the baby she lost.

"Oh, my God! What a miraculous sign! This time, I promise not to be ungrateful," she said out loud.

WITH A SECOND BABY on the way, Chelsea, who was seven months pregnant, decided she wanted to be closer to her parents. Over the next few weeks, they learned they were going to have a little boy, and they decided to name him Mace. They also found a house a few blocks away from her parents.

They successfully purchased the new place and quickly moved into their new home. Tabby's room was decorated, and Mace's nursery was all ready for his arrival. Their old house sold soon after the move, much to Chelsea's relief. She also had her new intern position in Information Systems Technology and would start in two short weeks. She finally felt like life was settling down.

As she was cooking dinner one night, Freddy came home in a bad mood. He was slamming doors, huffing, and puffing, and reeked of alcohol, which immediately annoyed Chelsea. She couldn't resist the urge to call him out on his childishness any longer and said, "Wow, looks like you went out with the boys after work!"

He glared at her and snapped. "Yes. I work, and I can go out with my friends."

She matched his attitude, glaring at him. "Well, good thing your pregnant wife takes care of work and the family, so you have time to go out with your friends!'"

He rushed over to her, got in her face, and screamed, "Then fucking quit work and take care of the family!"

This had been an ongoing fight between them in recent months. Freddy wanted her to quit her career, but she knew he had no clue how much anything costs or how to handle their finances.

She was the real breadwinner of the household and carrier of health insurance.

"Oh, okay, so you are going to step up and be the breadwinner finally and get us all insurance?" she fired right back, watching his nose flare-up.

He grabbed her by the shoulders near her neck and pushed her up against the wall. He kept her pinned and screamed, "Quit your job!"

"Ow, you're hurting me!" she shouted, trying to break free. "I'm not quitting my job. I can't, anyway." She looked at him dead in the eyes, and calmly spoke. "You need to leave now, or I will call the cops. I am pregnant, and this is not how I will be treated."

He let go of her neck and shoulders as he slammed his fists against the wall, close to her head, before lifting his fist. Chelsea knew he was about to hit her. He stopped as she curled away, her arms wrapped protectively around her stomach. His eyes had a fire in them as he stormed off into the garage.

She heard him rev up the SUV, a vehicle he recently bought from a friend without even consulting Chelsea. She stayed in her curled position with tears rolling down her face until she could smell dinner burning. She rushed back into the kitchen and saw Tabby looking at her from the hall.

"Mommy, baby Stacey wants to know why you are crying? Daddy mad?" she said in her baby voice. She didn't wait for an answer. She turned back around and continued to play with her baby doll, Stacey, and push her in a toy stroller.

Chelsea put the burnt dinner in the sink to soak. "Well, it looks like mommy needs to take you and baby Stacey to

McDonald's, and then we will go and see Aunt Jessica. Okay?" she declared as she picked Tabby up and hopped into the car.

Jessica was Tabby's godmother, and she loved her like her own. When they arrived at Jessica's house, Jessica immediately opened the door and hugged Chelsea. Tabby reached out for Jessica to hold her. "She is a little messy. We had McDonald's chicken nuggets on our way. Easy button, right?"

Jessica motioned for them to come into her apartment. "Well, this is a surprise!"

Then she looked at Chelsea. She saw the red marks Freddy had left on her shoulders and neck, and her red, bloodshot eyes.

"Oh, my God! Are you okay? What happened? Is the baby okay?" Jessica asked as she put her hand on Chelsea's baby bump.

Chelsea said, "Yes, the baby is fine, but Jess, I can't do it anymore. He threw me up against the wall because I wouldn't quit my job. I can't stay married. I have tried to love him. I've tried to look beyond it all, but his temper, partying, and selfishness is too much. I can't be with someone like … like … him. He is constantly smoking, violent, and never helps, and here I am, pregnant with a toddler. I am barely twenty-one years old."

Jessica gave her an empathetic smile and said, "He was mentioning finishing the basement. Maybe he can go from the garage to the basement each day. That way, you both have the new home but are separated. It worked better when he worked nights, and you were days. Right?"

Chelsea nodded, and Jessica continued. "Now that you are both working days and actually see each other at night, it sounds like it's becoming toxic for you."

They talked for a couple of hours until Chelsea looked over at Tabby and saw her eyes looking pretty heavy. She smiled and picked her up. "Jess, I'd better go get her into bed. Thank you for your advice. I'll call you, and I'll talk to him about the basement tomorrow. I think that is a good solution. It isn't marriage, but at least we are both in the home for the children."

Jessica walked Chelsea out, gave Tabby hugs and kisses, and said, "You be good for your mom. I love you!"

She turned to Chelsea and said, "Chels, it will be okay. You have been through more, but if he touches you again, throw his ass in jail. I mean it!"

Chelsea nodded her head to Jessica as she brushed the chicken nugget breading off of the car seat, buckled Tabby in, and kissed her on the cheek.

"Maybe we will do a bath in the morning, so we both can go to bed," she whispered, smiling, as Tabby's eyes began to close.

THE NEXT DAY, FREDDY walked in the door. Chelsea was sitting on the couch, watching TV with Tabby. He walked over to kiss them both, and Chelsea turned her head away from him. She could smell the alcohol and smoke on him the second he walked into the room.

"We need to talk," Chelsea stated, and she stood up and motioned for him to move upstairs away from Tabby's little ears.

They both walked upstairs into the master bedroom. She sat on the rocking chair, which she had assembled a few days earlier.

He sat on the edge of the bed across from her. Chelsea sighed as she began what she knew would be a life-altering decision. "I want a divorce. I'm seven months pregnant. I start a new position at work soon. I unpacked this entire house alone. I take care of our daughter, and I signed up for online college classes today. I refuse to live another moment with someone whose life ambition is to party with friends and watch his wife do all the work. I'm getting a loan to finish the basement tomorrow, or at least finish a room for you to stay in until you find something else. This way, both kids will still see you. I can't bring another baby into this horrible marriage. I don't want the kids to grow up seeing how you are with your anger, alcohol issues, cutting yourself, fighting at work, and barely taking care of yourself. Please know this is a decision I have made and not a negotiation. I have thought about it for years."

Freddy's eyes were wide, and his mouth slightly open as he gritted his teeth while Chelsea was talking. Every time he started to get angry, she would tilt her head, challenging him with a look and a hand to keep him quiet.

After a long pause, he stuttered, "But you canceled my vasectomy last week because you wanted to continue to build our family. Why do you want a divorce now?" The words were impacting him now, and tears were welling up in his eyes.

Chelsea looked at him with tears in her eyes and explained, "No, I canceled your vasectomy last week because we are not going to have a future, and I don't want to be the reason you don't have children with someone else. It was clear to me when you pinned me up against the wall last night. That was the final nail in the coffin."

Freddy looked stunned and said, "I barely touched you."

Chelsea revealed her shoulder and neck. "Yes, I have the bruise marks and fingerprints from you, barely touching me. You already said you can't watch our daughter because you are afraid you are going to beat her or shake her to death. You just got in trouble at work for pinning a coworker to a desk by the throat and put on suspension for two days without pay. This is not a discussion. I don't want to be married to you, and I don't want to live the life you have given me. I don't care if I am pregnant right now—I'm already raising Tabby by myself. I can raise a second on my own, too. I've already had practice raising her and you for the last four years."

Tabby started to walk up the stairs to join her parents, so Chelsea rushed out to give Freddy space.

Chelsea picked Tabby up. "Do you want to go for a walk?"

Tabby, of course, was excited to sit in the stroller as she grinned and started bouncing in Chelsea's arms.

Chelsea could hear Freddy throwing things around the bedroom and swearing. Through the closed door, she heard him mutter, "Fucking bitch."

Chelsea was in the garage, putting Tabby in the stroller, as Freddy rushed past them and jumped into the SUV, almost hitting the stroller and Tabby on his way out. *Seriously, he has no disregard for anyone.*

Tabby yelled, "Bye, Daddy!"

Chelsea looked down at Tabby, relieved that she was okay, before laughing and saying, "Yep. Bye, Daddy. Now let's go for a walk. Then let's try and eat something called vegetables when we get home. They are almost like chicken nuggets, but, um . . . different."

Chelsea finished buckling her into the stroller and kissed her cheek. As she was buckling her in, she realized that bending down was a little harder this pregnancy. "Wow! Mama needs to walk with you more. She is getting out of shape and has a big belly in her way."

Tabby poked her belly and said, "Baby?"

Chelsea looked at Tabby and gushed, "Yep. Your baby brother, Mace."

Chelsea then suggested, "Hey, let's go to the park to let you run around."

At the park, Tabby was screaming and playing, finally not being a bully to the other children in the park. Chelsea loved her daughter, but that baby girl's sass and attitude were border-line troublesome for a toddler. She was a three-year-old bully. Chelsea would often say to people, "It's a good thing she's cute."

I'm so glad that the nine months of pregnancy is going fast. Having Freddy live in the basement is not ideal. I hope he doesn't remember that today is our anniversary. Who am I joking?

Tabby ran over and jumped on Chelsea's lap. Chelsea had immediate pain, and she felt like she had either peed her pants or possibly her water broke.

"Um, Tabby, it is time to go," Chelsea sighed while holding her belly and bending down to pick Tabby up. She put her into the stroller as she started to throw a tantrum, the kind of tantrum where everyone in the park looks to see whether the mother is abusing the child or the child is overly dramatic.

"Tabby, that is enough! Mommy is feeling sick, and we need to go home. I think you will get to meet your brother today,"

Chelsea demanded as Tabby continued to kick and scream in the air.

Chelsea continued to hurt and was feeling more and more water leak out with every step she took. By the time they arrived at the house, she was having intense contractions.

She rushed to the phone to call her mom. "Hi, mom, can you meet me at the hospital and watch Tabby? I'm in labor."

Her mom stammered, "Yes."

Chelsea waddled to grab her prepacked bag. She threw in some extra things for Tabby and drove them to the hospital. Tabby was still throwing a tantrum. It was like she was trying to get all the attention she could before her mommy was busy with the new baby.

The nurse was sweet and pulled Tabby away from Chelsea to let her change into the hospital gown. The back pain and labor were getting intense, and she had already been told that the baby would be over eight pounds. She changed into her hospital gown as her family showed up.

They looked at her and chuckled. "Looks like you are going to have another night-owl baby."

Chelsea looked at the clock. It was already 10:37 P.M. She laughed through the pain. "Well, clearly, I'm not going to raise any morning people."

At 2:45 A.M. the next morning, Chelsea and the world opened their arms to a healthy, ten-pound, twenty-three-inch long baby boy, Mace.

Chapter 14
PLAYER IN THE WORKPLACE

—————

*C*HELSEA WAS BACK TO work in her new department, criminal investigation. When she was introduced to who she would be working with, *Oh my! At this new job, the men seem a little overly friendly. After my experience at the tire shop, I have no choice but to be pretty blunt toward any not-so-subtle pickup lines.*

One gentleman, Garrett, was relentless in his flirting with her. She often said to him, "Aren't you married?"

Garrett would laugh it off and say, "Well, I'm separated, like you. I'll file today if I can take you out." Usually, that was followed by a wink or him slipping her his phone number.

"If you haven't filed, then you are married, not separated! I might be legally separated, but I have a baby, toddler, new job, and a new home, and I am definitely not looking for anything else," she told him with a smart-ass smile, making it known she was not interested. When he gave her his number, she tossed it in the garbage right in front of him.

The problem with Garrett was that his office was next to hers and she had to ask him questions all day. In fact, other people would give her questions to ask him as well, because he was so accommodating to answer her. She loathed knowing the entire office knew he had the hots for her and that they both had to rely on each other for specific sets of data, making it impossible to finish a big job without seeing or talking to one another. They would even have to carry equipment, go to different locations, and enter the data daily.

ONE TIME ON THE way to another location, Garrett drove down the wrong road.

Chelsea noticed he was going in the wrong direction and asked, "Where are you going?"

Her pulse started to race, and she immediately panicked. She couldn't lose her job, and she certainly was not going to go to a hotel or something with a coworker.

He looked at her and grinned at her anxiety. "Relax. I'm taking you flying."

Chelsea looked over at him, puzzled, and asked, "Taking me where?"

He smiled mischievously at her and replied, "It is five minutes away, and it will not take any longer than a lunch break. I have lunch on the plane for us."

Chelsea had never had anyone do anything considerate or plan something like this for her before. She had only flown once before and had never been in a smaller plane, which made her extremely nervous.

Garrett started walking around the plane, doing checks. She sat in the plane, looking around at all the controls. It was a small four-seater, a Cessna or something like that.

Chelsea's stomach was on fire because all she could think about was dying. She imagined hearing her family talking about why she was with Garrett in the first place.

This certainly wasn't my plan, and I am kind of being kidnapped in a sense, she thought to herself, laughing inside about how she agreed to drive to the location together to save gas.

It was the most romantic date she had ever been on. No one, especially Freddy, had ever been thoughtful enough to surprise her.

As she was watching him walk around the plane, she was checking him out. He was really tall, with dark hair and piercing blue eyes. She couldn't believe he was nine years older than she was. She had always pictured a 30-year-old man as much older, because due to Freddy's drugs, alcohol, and smoking, his five years older seemed more than Garrett's nine years.

Freddy definitely looks older and more laborious than Garrett.

She also loved that Garrett was tall, *I can wear heels around him.*

She was 5'9", but in heels, she seemed to tower over most men, including Freddy. There was something about a man taller than her that made her feel petite and more feminine.

Garrett returned to the plane and hopped in the pilot seat. *He seems comfortable.*

He put his hand on her shoulder and handed her a headset. They both put on the earphones, which allowed them to speak to the air traffic controller and to one another.

"Are you nervous?" he asked her with a smile and a wink.

Chelsea nodded. "Uh-huh!"

"Don't worry, I've only crashed once," Garrett joked.

Chelsea's eyes got big, her mouth opened, and then she noticed he had a smirk on his face, so she punched his arm and said, "Not funny!"

He started the engines and began talking on the radio as he taxied for takeoff. He announced he was doing some touch and goes, which he later explained were takeoff and landings.

"I intend to fly around the city to see this beautiful lady's house," he said as he winked at her.

Chapter 15
WOLF IN SHEEP'S CLOTHING

———

AFTER WORK, CHELSEA SCRAMBLED to get home to her kids. Both of them were always starving by the time she picked them up from the babysitter. Once home, she rushed to prepare a bottle for Mace and gave Tabby a snack to hold her over as she began to make dinner.

Freddy came upstairs and kissed the kids. *He is acting weird. I wonder if he has been following me or something. He is overly sweet and seems to be up to something.* Then her mind wandered on to thoughts of Garrett. *That flight was so incredible. What a romantic man.*

She could feel her face flush, and she had butterflies in her stomach. Garrett was so quick to make her smile, and she realized that no man had done that since before Freddy.

Freddy looked at her and said, "Why don't we go and refinance the car in my name? Then, you can take the paid-off SUV.

It will help you financially and also help for when you refinance the house out of my name."

Chelsea glanced up from cooking with a shocked look on her face. "Oh my! That would be awesome. It will better for the winter months coming up. My car really scares me in the snow. Now that I'm driving around two babies, it is a good idea."

Freddy said, "Well, good. How about your mom watches the kids, and we go to the bank now?"

Chelsea looked at him, "Nah, we can do it this weekend. I just picked them up, and I don't want to leave them again. Plus, the bank is probably closed already."

He rolled his eyes and sighed. "Okay." Then turned around and walked back downstairs.

Chelsea mumbled under her breath, "And there he is!" *Hmm, last time he was acting crazy like this, I ended up with Tabby, but I know that would never happen to me again. I'm lifetimes ahead of where I was four years ago.*

Chelsea went and put the kids in the bath. Mace still hated the tub, but Tabby would splash and entertain herself all day if Chelsea would let her.

Why do I keep thinking about Garrett, and why am I so damn intrigued by him? I need to do something that makes me stop thinking about him. He is still married, for hell's sakes, and so am I.

The other problem was that her mom also worked with him. *I'll finish this project, and I won't see him again,* she told herself, but in her mind, she pictured someone that would treat her well, sweep her off her feet, and rescue her from her current hell.

IN THE NEXT SEVERAL weeks, Chelsea tried to distance herself from Garrett. *He is the last thing I need right now. I need Freddy to move out already.*

Freddy was like another messy child at home, and she had her hands full already. Everything about Freddy bugged her—his smell, his demeanor, his look, and his mess.

She decided to proceed and do as she pleased. She was hoping it would push him over the edge. *Maybe if I piss him off enough, he will leave already. Life isn't hard enough with me now.*

She went and got her navel pierced and scheduled an appointment for a breast augmentation.

"What the fuck, Chels! Why?" Freddy yelled as he flipped out.

Chelsea explained, "Why not? I have stretch marks on my breasts from having two babies and three pregnancies. Why not fill those right back up? Plus, what I do isn't any of your business. We are legally separated and getting divorced. How is that house hunting coming?"

Freddy looked at her and said, "You are a complete bitch!" And then he stormed off.

"Yes, I am. Thank you for noticing. And while you are running away, why don't you pack," she snapped back.

CHELSEA WAS HURRYING OUT of the house to meet Jessica for Chelsea's breast augmentation surgery as Freddy stood in the door and hissed, "Chelsea, I forbid you to do this."

Chelsea was taken aback and explained, "Forbid away. I'm doing whatever I want. I'm done pleasing you."

This time, he realized Chelsea was indeed done and sneered, "Fine. I will move out and be gone by the time you get home."

Chelsea softened and whispered, "That would be best for us both."

The finality of Chelsea's words hit, *At least I will have time off work, and I can avoid seeing Garrett and Freddy. Working from home will be useful as I process it all.*

DAYS AFTER SIGNING THE divorce papers and receiving the title to the SUV, the SUV broke down, which left her stranded on the side of the road with the children.

She had no idea who to call, so she called Garrett, who came to her rescue.

When it was towed into the shop, the mechanic looked at her, puzzled. "Why do you have this vehicle? I told Freddy a month and a half ago that it would break down if he didn't repair several problems."

Hmm, so him asking for the car and then giving me the SUV wasn't to help me financially. Well, at least I know now why Freddy was nice that day. He was making sure I had the broken SUV all along. What a loser!

SHE WENT INTO THE shop bathroom, fell to her knees, and broke down into tears. Once again, because of Freddy, she was crying and financially suffering.

Chapter 16
PLANNED PAPERS

⌒

A FEW WEEKS LATER, AT work, Garrett and Chelsea were in the utility locker room at the warehouse. Garrett looked over at her and handed her a paper.

"What is this, more work for me?" she said as she grabbed the paper and began to look at it. Her eyes opened wide to see that they were his divorce papers. She chuckled, "What makes you think this means anything to me?"

He snatched the paper from her hands playfully, pushed her up against a mainframe computer, and kissed her. He kissed her with more passion than she had ever experienced. She instantly had butterflies.

THAT NIGHT, WITH THE help of her mom, she updated her resume. *It isn't that I don't love to see him daily, but with the thought of an inter-work relationship and the awkwardness of telling my manager, I think I should leave that position.*

Garrett was in a high position and had connections, but Chelsea was intelligent and hardworking. She didn't want anyone to think she moved up the ladder, because of some guy. *No man will ever take credit for my accomplishments.*

She emailed her resume later that night to a few companies. A couple days later, she was offered a job making tax software.

I am so nervous about starting a new job and go to a small company, but I'm excited to not be involved with the government. Something is liberating about not following in your family's footsteps.

CHELSEA YAWNED AS HER eyes flickered into darkness due to exhaustion. Her old coworkers Monica and Sarah, often came over after work with Garrett. The kids would play, and they would have wine and catch up on their days at work. Monica, Garrett and Sarah all still worked together. Chelsea felt she wasn't missing out when they visited.

"Everyone at my new job is either family, a neighbor, or someone in the family's church," Chelsea explained. "I love the company, but clearly, I am quite out of place."

Garrett was practically living in the house with Chelsea. He hadn't completely moved in yet, but that was the plan. He could help her with the bills, and they would see where their relationship would go. She refinanced the home and put it solely in her name so that Freddy was not tied to the house anymore.

She kept Garrett's name off of the home because she was able to qualify by herself and felt that it was a huge accomplishment.

Most of her life, she felt like her voice was taken away, and that little feat made her feel like she was in control of her surroundings.

Freddy was sporadic in the children's lives, and that was fine by Chelsea. She still wasn't entirely comfortable with him being alone with the kids. She had already taken him to court because Mace had come home from Freddy's house, unable to breathe. The cigarette smoke from Freddy and his newly pregnant girlfriend were hard on a toddler with asthma.

Garrett finally had his divorce finalized, which was an ugly fight between him and his wife. They had been married for ten years, had two kids, and his ex-wife blamed Chelsea for destroying their marriage.

LIFE SEEMED TO BE going well with Chelsea's blossoming relationship with Garrett. "Baby, do you think your mom can babysit for us to have a date night, all dressed up?" Garrett asked.

"I'm sure she would love time with the kids. We do need a date night," she gushed, *I love that he is so romantic.*

Chelsea went and borrowed a fancy dress from Jessica, and it took all the energy she had to get dolled up. *Something about dressing up makes you instantly feel better.*

A limo pulled up to pick them up, and she was in shock that Garrett went all out for their date night. They went to a nice restaurant and then to her favorite places to see the Christmas lights.

"What a perfect and relaxing evening," Chelsea told Garrett.

He popped open some champagne open in the limo, and she started laughing as the cork hit the ceiling, "Did you know I have never had champagne?"

He laughed and said, "Well, you are only 22 years old."

Chelsea smiled and exclaimed, "True. Why do I feel so much older than I am? I have an old soul, I guess, and years of experience."

They held each other and continued to sip the champagne as the car parked, overlooking the city. The lights sparkled below, and the stars were bright in the night sky. He held her hand and got down on one knee and asked, "Chels, will you marry me?"

He held up a massive diamond ring.

Chelsea was shocked and put her hands over her mouth. She then looked down at him, pulled him up off his knee, and gushed, "Absolutely."

Chapter 17
THE GREAT GETAWAY

CHELSEA WAS SCREECHING WITH glee and excitement as she told Jessica the news. She planned on calling all of her friends the next day, but of course, Jessica was the first to hear.

"Hi, Jessica!" said Chelsea in her upbeat and sassy voice.

Jessica gasped. "Oh, no! What's going on?" She could always read Chelsea's tones and expressions.

"Well, Garrett proposed, and I said yes. Am I insane? He is nine years older than me, has two kids, and is recently divorced from a ten-year marriage. I'm in the same boat with two kids and barely being divorced."

Jessica started laughing and said, "Well, my advice is to make it a longer engagement. At least this time, you can actually plan it without it being a shotgun wedding like you did with Freddy."

Chelsea was rolling on the floor and giggled. "So, you are telling me to be traditional?"

They talked about the proposal and future wedding plans.

"Of course, you are my maid of honor again, okay?" Chelsea asked.

"Well, of course, duh!" Jessica said, laughing.

"I'm thinking of a summer wedding on a beach at some remote location. I want the wedding I have always dreamed of this time around." Chelsea explained in vivid detail. "I want red, white, and pink plumerias, like in my dreams, and a white gown that is fitted to show off all of my hard work losing weight after my three pregnancies."

Jessica chuckled. "Don't forget a cake that doesn't fall the second you say, 'I do.'"

"Oh my hell! How did I forget about that? That was an omen to a doomed marriage. Right?" Chelsea laughed. "This time, though, instead of gaining weight and worrying the dress won't fit, I have the opposite problem. I have no idea why I keep losing weight. Sure, I work out a ton, but some weeks I lose five pounds doing nothing. I desperately need a vacation."

They hung up, and Chelsea walked into the room to talk to Garrett.

"I was talking to Jess, and I really think I need a vacation. I'm dropping weight like crazy, and it has been a hell of a year. Plus, I think we both need time away."

"I agree. You work so hard. Let's go to Vegas. I will fly us both there. You can actually rest from the four children, Freddy drama, new job, and just life. It will allow me to get my flight hours in, and I'll be the first one to take you to Vegas," Garrett stated.

She was soon to marry someone and have a two-year-old, five-year-old, seven-year-old, and nine-year-old in their household. She absolutely loved all of the children, but they were a lot of work.

Garrett's little boy, Luke, who was seven, was a handful. He was a whiny brat most days, and he would bite, spit, and punch anything or anyone in sight.

Lucy, his daughter, was a pretty good girl and mature for her nine years.

Tabby was five now and started having immense jealousy toward Lucy and the other siblings. One time, she grabbed scissors and went after each of them individually, trying to stab them. She succeeded in stabbing the two boys, but luckily the only scissors she could grab were blunt.

Mace was turning two years old and was, by far, the most relaxed child. If toys were taken away, he would move on to another toy. If Luke punched him, he would walk away and not even cry. It amazed Chelsea at how mean Luke and Tabby were to him, but it didn't seem to faze him at all. He would sit happily on Chelsea's lap to read a book or go off to play by himself.

Besides being a busy mother of four young children, working full-time, planning a wedding, and rearranging rooms for the children, Chelsea had also signed up to be the associate soccer coordinator for children under six, which consisted of fifty-six teams. She even decided to sign up to coach Tabby's soccer team and be an assistant coach for Luke's soccer team.

"I think if I get Tabby and Luke into sports, we can bond, and it should help them release their anger and hate for everything," Chelsea was telling Garrett. "Somehow, I only require two hours of sleep anymore. It'll help keep my boredom to a minimum."

She needed the Vegas trip with her fiancé. *Fiancé. How weird is it that? He is my fiancé.*

She had to admit that although she loved her children and his, she really did need a break from them. *This will be the first vacation where I have left the children. I'm so glad it is only for three days.*

THEY GOT INTO THE plane, Garrett did the checks, and she put on the headphones. She felt like a flying pro by now, but this trip was longer than any others. The plane had to land to refuel in St. George, Utah.

The flight into Las Vegas was like nothing Chelsea had ever seen, with all of the lights and homes and the Las Vegas Strip in the background. "It is so majestic," she said through her headphones.

When they landed, they took a taxi to the hotel and changed into fancier clothes. Chelsea had never been to Vegas other than for soccer tournaments. It was a beautiful town full of lights, and the casino had a perfume smell she couldn't put her finger on.

She wore a form-fitting lace dress and silver high heels. She put on the diamond earrings and necklace that Garrett had bought her for Valentine's Day. She felt like she was utterly glowing as she peered out of the window to see the Las Vegas Strip.

However, she remembered she needed to call the children, as she grabbed her phone to see it was dead.

"Garrett? I need to borrow your phone to check in on the kids. Mine is dead, and I have no idea where in our luggage the charger is. Is that okay?" she yelled to him in the bathroom.

He was brushing his teeth and said, "Uh, huh." Chelsea grabbed his phone to see a few missed calls and texts from Monica, the girl who used to hang out with them both after work and still worked with Garrett.

Well, that's odd, I wonder if they have a work emergency.

"Garrett? Monica keeps trying to call you. Maybe something with work?" she yelled as he shrugged his shoulders.

Then she saw a text message from Monica come in that read, "Call me when she isn't around."

Just then, he walked out of the bathroom, and Chelsea asked, "Why is Monica calling you? And what is this?" She pointed out the text message.

Garrett grabbed the phone, looked down at it, and stuttered, "It's likely the surprise I have planned for you. I asked her for suggestions."

Chelsea looked at him and stated, "Oh! I see. Okay, but why don't you talk to Jessica about that stuff? Next to Monica coming over a few times after work, and us working together, she really doesn't know me at all." Garrett nodded his head in agreement. Chelsea was confused about why Garrett would ask Monica anything since she stopped inviting her old coworkers over months ago when she found out Monica had been doing drugs in the bathroom.

He grabbed her hand, kissed her, and said, "Let's go to the MGM happy hour, my love."

Chapter 18
NOT EVERYTHING STAYS IN VEGAS

*C*HELSEA WOKE UP FEELING like a train had run her over. As she stumbled to the bathroom, she was stepping over clothing, shoes, pillows, and blankets.

"Wow!" she muttered under her breath, holding her head. "We clearly tore up the town. Too bad I don't remember it. Why don't I remember it? I need water."

She walked into the kitchen, grabbed a glass, and filled it with water. She was gulping down glass after glass when she looked over and saw a paper. She picked it up and saw it was a marriage certificate. Then she saw drunken photos of them at a chapel. "Oh, my God! Are these wedding photos? It is a chapel. What happened?" she screamed out loud.

She ran over to Garrett, shaking him to wake him up and asked, "What is this?"

Garrett looked at her with one eye, still half-closed, and said, "It's our marriage certificate, silly."

"Why are there wedding photos and a marriage certificate? I don't remember any of this," Chelsea sobbed in a complete panic.

He looked at her and laughed, "Well, I told you to never let anyone give you a drink, but you had fun and were lots of fun."

"We got married?" she cried with her mouth open wide and tears in her eyes.

"Yes, babe, you agreed with me that we should go to the chapel and get married, so it was one less thing for you to do and stress about," he said, sitting up and laughing at her panic.

"No! I wanted our perfect wedding. Not some wedding I don't remember," she sobbed with tears rolling down her cheeks.

Garrett grabbed her and stated, "It's just a piece of paper. I was already committed to you before this paper. We will have a good honeymoon. How about Hawaii? You've always wanted to go, and I will look for flights today. We can leave as soon as next week. It's just a piece of paper, Chels."

Chelsea finally started to calm down, still drinking glass after glass of water.

Garrett sprung out of bed, grabbed his computer, and frantically started looking for flights to Hawaii. "We can even go scuba diving. We haven't gone anywhere since we were certified," he said as he peered above his computer.

"I don't remember my wedding. Oh, my hell! I don't remember my wedding. I feel like a foolish little girl," she cried to him.

"Baby, I wonder if someone spiked your drink last night because you didn't have that many drinks. Vegas indeed has much stronger drinks than Utah, but you seemed with it for the most part. It's okay. I'll remember for both of us," he said, trying to calm her. "Let's go to the pool and relax."

She gladly agreed, changed into her bikini, and grabbed towels. She walked out to find Garrett on the balcony talking on his phone. He spoke for a few minutes, and then he looked over at her and hurried off the phone.

"Who was that?" Chelsea asked.

"Just work," he said as he grabbed his swim trunks to change. Then he came up to her and grabbed her butt, kissed her hard, and held her hand to walk to the pool.

The pool was a clothing-optional adult pool, which was nothing Chelsea had ever experienced or wanted to experience. Sure, she had a great body and brand-new perky breasts, but she was too modest to walk around without a top or in a thong, which was fine by Garrett, who was extremely jealous when guys looked at her.

He often commented that she looked so young, fit, and beautiful, and he was an old, skinny, tall dude.

Chelsea would laugh and say, "You are handsome, baby!"

At the pool, Chelsea had her first mimosa, which was champagne with orange juice, she found out. Everyone told her it would help make her feel better after a night of drinking too much.

Garrett showed her his phone and asked, "So next weekend—Hawaii?"

Chelsea looked over and said, "I'll check at work, but since we aren't in peak tax season, it should be fine.

WHEN THEY RETURNED TO Utah, they decided to tell everyone they decided to elope. Chelsea talked to her family and Jessica about how they eloped. She then asked her mom if she would watch the kids again for their honeymoon to Hawaii.

Chelsea's mom stammered, "Oh, wow! I thought you wanted a big wedding, but your dad and I couldn't handle all the stress either, and we eloped, too. I would love to have the children longer. Sadie and I can take them to the newly opened planetarium."

Tabby and Mace cheered at that comment and swarmed their grandma and Sadie.

Chelsea's dad giggled as he declared, "I'm going golfing." Then he turned his focus back to the basketball game on the television.

Chelsea looked over at Jessica, who had an inquisitive look on her face as she pursed her lips.

I love that girl, but she does not have a poker face.

Jessica motioned by tilting her head for Chelsea to go to another room to talk. They walked into Chelsea's old bedroom and shut the door, and Jessica insisted, "Bullshit, Chelsea. You didn't decide to elope after you wanted the perfect wedding. What happened?"

"Great question. I did Vegas with a hangover to boot. I'm so upset I can't have my dream wedding now," Chelsea sighed.

Jessica consoled her. "Maybe you can do a reception and still get dressed up in your new wedding dress?"

Chelsea groaned. "It isn't the same since it will be after the fact. I'm so embarrassed I was that drunk girl who doesn't remember her own wedding."

Chapter 19
JUST GOT MAUI'ED

ON THE PARASAILING BOAT, they picked a harness that said "Just Maui'ed" with plumerias all around it.

"That's a sign. They put us in the perfect harness," she said to Garrett.

He giggled. "Oh, you and your plumerias."

"Hey, look!" she said matter-of-factly. "My plumerias and dreams are signs that God and spirits are always around me. We went scuba diving together and ran into a bunch of fishermen who were feeding sharks. You cut your hand in the cave, and there was a reason you weren't shark bait." She chuckled. "At that point, I was definitely questioning that vow about for better or for worst, so don't mock my plumeria obsession and looking for spiritual signs. Something saved us."

"Okay, you might have a point," he agreed.

Chelsea couldn't believe it. She was in Maui on her honeymoon. She felt so happy that she was finally in a happy marriage. *Even if it is only one week of marriage, it still was better than the years with Freddy.*

THAT NIGHT AT THE luau, her phone rang.

"Oh, Gare. I hate to say this, but it was work. Someone had to have surgery, so the day after I get back, I have to leave for San Francisco for a trade show. I feel like such a bad mom for leaving the children for so long," she sighed.

Garrett looked at her and smiled. "Go! I have everything covered."

She was so floored he was so willing to watch the kids and be there when she was away. He was already there more than Freddy was in the last four years.

"THE WHOLE HONEYMOON WAS fun, but I sure am glad to be home with my babies after five days," she told her mom after they returned.

"There was a tornado downtown while you were gone," her mom explained.

"A tornado in Utah? Wow!" Chelsea replied.

Her family described how suddenly it hit. After several minutes of talking, Chelsea asked, "How were the kiddos?"

"They were all great, except Tabby. She was so naughty! It was like she was possessed," Chelsea's mom said with concern.

Chelsea looked at her and said, "I'm so sorry. I don't know what is wrong with her. She does seem like she is possessed most days. I'm putting her in dance to work off some more of her attitude. Hopefully, she'll outgrow it." She paused for a moment before continuing. "Well, thanks for watching them. I fly out in the morning, so I need to get these kiddos to bed," she said, hugging them as she ushered them out the door.

That night she did laundry and moved it from one suitcase to another one.

IN SAN FRANCISCO, SHE finally arrived to join her coworkers, and she was welcomed with open arms. Others described her as the "technical people-person." It always made her laugh when anybody was surprised at how technical she was, yet it seemed to come naturally to her.

Chelsea hurried and sat down on a chair and took a moment to compose herself. *Why am I always feeling like I'm going to pass out? Losing weight rapidly, heart freaking out, shaking all the time—what is wrong with me?*

"Chels, you don't look so good," her boss stated.

"You know. I've been sick for a while, but maybe I have jet lag?" she replied.

Her boss began to worry and said with concern, "Tomorrow, let's have you fly out two days early and get looked at by a doctor. You look really thin and pale, and you're shaking. Please don't take that the wrong way, but you are not you."

"No offense taken. I do need to go to the doctor. I keep losing weight, and I can't seem to eat enough. I know it is a good problem to have, but I'm even worried about it. I feel like it is out of my control. I'll fly in early and surprise Garrett and then go to the doctor," she agreed, smiling.

Jessica picked her up from the airport and took her to the house. She waved goodbye and walked into the house, excited to surprise Garrett.

As she walked into the entryway, she heard noises upstairs. She sprinted up the stairs.

She opened her bedroom door to find Garrett having sex with Monica.

She immediately felt rage rush through her body. Garrett looked over to see her and sprung to his feet and over to her. "You son of a bitch!" she yelled as she slapped him so hard he went flying back.

Monica ripped the sheet from off the bed and wrapped it around her as she grabbed what clothes she could find. She sprinted past Chelsea and stammered, "I'm sorry, Chels."

Chelsea lost all cool and started screaming every cuss word that came into her head. "I'm getting an annulment! You are a cheating prick."

My ideal marriage was all a lie. I was lied to. I was deceived by my husband and an old friend.

She started shoving his clothes into a bag, crying and yelling out loud, "You prick! You were even cheating before we got married. That's why she was texting and calling you in Las Vegas. You are a son of a bitch. How could you?! Get out now!"

Garrett started gathering what he could, and through the tears, sobbed, "Babe! It was stupid, and I don't want to leave."

Chelsea glared at him and tossed a bag with his belongings in it at him with impressive force. "Get out now!"

She picked up the phone and talked to her lawyer to start the paperwork for an annulment. Chelsea was embarrassed, and she felt like a fool wondering how she was going to explain it to people. She had already changed her name when she returned back from Vegas, and she was still coaching Garrett's son in soccer.

How can this keep happening to me? Maybe my mom can watch the kids tonight while I process everything. I can't have them see me like this.

She picked up the phone and asked, "Mom? Can you watch the children for a little bit longer? I came home today, but I don't feel well, and I am hoping I can lie down."

"Of course, honey! Do you need me to do anything else?" Chelsea's mom asked.

"No. My boss gave me the day off tomorrow to go to the doctor. I'll get on some antibiotics or something, and I'll come to get the children after that if that is okay. Thank you for watching them," she said as she hung up the phone.

She dialed Jessica and immediately started sobbing. "Jessica, oh my God, I feel like the biggest fool. I caught Garrett and Monica in bed a few minutes ago. I now have to tell everyone I failed at another marriage at twenty-two years old."

"I'm on my way over," Jessica said, concerned.

Jessica was recently engaged, and Chelsea loved seeing her so happy. She had visions of them both double dating and the four of them being one, big, happy, extended family.

Jessica immediately showed up and lifted Chelsea up off of the floor while Chelsea was crying. As usual, she was able to listen and give sound advice.

"I'm going to lie down. How about we talk tomorrow when my head isn't spinning? The kids can watch movies, and we can spend time drinking our mommy juice," Chelsea said after an hour of talking.

"Sounds like a plan. You do look like you don't feel good. Try to rest. I love you," Jessica replied as she headed toward the door.

I need a nap, but first, I need to write a letter. She began writing a letter to Monica's husband, telling him about Garrett and Monica.

"Why should anyone else be lied to?" she said out loud as she walked the letter to the mailbox.

Chapter 20
THE SEASON OF CHANGE

IT WAS SATURDAY MORNING, and Chelsea still hadn't found time or energy to go to the doctor. "I'll go next week," she replied when her mom called to ask about it.

She was dreading coaching soccer that morning. She knew she was going to see Garrett at his son's soccer game, and she didn't know how she was going to contain her anger or pain.

Chelsea walked onto the field to start coaching. *Thank God! I don't see the prick,* as she looked around and saw Garrett's ex-wife glaring at her.

"If looks could kill!" she whispered to herself.

I can only imagine what he did to her. If I wasn't sent home from my trip early, I might have never known. Chelsea was filled with trepidation and lost in thought when she noticed the game was about to start. She gathered the boys in for a huddle and insisted, "Go have fun, but remember to work as a team." She grabbed Luke as they were running onto the field and hugged him one last time.

As Chelsea coached the boys, she could still feel the glares from Garrett's ex-wife. She wanted so badly to say, "Fine! You were so right, and I'm sorry for all you thought I did."

Chelsea knew she definitely had an emotional affair with Garrett before his separation, and the guilt had been crushing her. They hadn't started a physical relationship at that point, even though she was blamed for it in Garrett's court documents. *At least the season is almost over, and I'll never have to see her again. Maybe I can write her an apology letter when it is all done.*

The boys were ahead by two goals. Chelsea walked over to talk to the coach. "I'm feeling really light-headed. If I still feel bad by the next quarter, can you finish coaching and refereeing without me?" she asked as Garrett came over.

She put her hand to Garrett's face, shook her head, and ran onto the field to finish the game.

As she was running down the field with the team, she felt something pop in her neck. It was a feeling she had never experienced before, like part of her neck had popped.

"Oh, no! What was that? A kink?" she said, as she stopped running, she felt her neck, which had a bump. She pushed on the bump and then collapsed on the sidelines.

She woke up feeling disoriented. She felt her neck, and the bump was gone.

The boys came rushing over along with the coach and Garrett to check on her. They helped her up, and as she stood slowly, she sighed. "I must have the flu. Lots of traveling."

She turned and looked at the coach and handed him her whistle. "You got this?" she asked. He nodded.

She walked to her car and prayed she wouldn't pass out again. "All I want to do is go home and lie down. I'm so tired. Maybe I'm getting a migraine," she said as she sat in the car.

It was a rough week, and her stress level was intense, so a migraine would make sense. She held onto the steering wheel, trying to get her eyes to focus. She looked into the rear-view mirror to see her neck. It was almost purple and had a significant bump on it. She pushed on the mass again and got lightheaded.

"I'm dreading going to urgent care, but something is clearly wrong with a big purple bump on my neck," she said, trying to make herself laugh at the irony of her week.

As she started the car, Garrett jumped in the passenger seat and turned the car off. Chelsea glared at him and hissed. "I don't have time for your bullshit, Garrett. I don't feel good, and I'm going to urgent care."

Garrett nodded, moving his head back to prevent her from slapping him again, and said, "I know, and I'm driving you, so switch me seats."

THE RIDE TO THE urgent care center seemed like a blur. Chelsea didn't know whether it was because she fell asleep or all the stress she was under, or maybe it was the pain of feeling like her heart had been punctured a million times over by tiny pins. She knew she was not in good shape.

The nurses immediately took her into an examining room and grabbed the ultrasound machine. "I would like to run some tests, but I think it would be better to send you to the ER where they will expedite them," the doctor explained.

She nodded her head and didn't really care what they did if she could only close her eyes and sleep through it.

IN THE ER, THEY put jelly on her neck and moved the controller around. They began whispering to one another and rushed out of the room. Chelsea closed her eyes to rest and avoid seeing Garrett staring at her.

Moments later, she opened her eyes to see that two more doctors were in her room now. They all looked at the machine and simultaneously said, "Thyroid!"

Chelsea had no idea what a thyroid was. "I think some glands became swollen and popped, or my neck kinked," she whispered in a groggy voice.

"It will be okay, Chels. We are going to help you into a wheelchair and take you back for more tests," the nurse said.

They helped her into a wheelchair, and she barely sat down when the nurse started rushing out of the room. *Wow. Either my head is spinning, or this nurse is walking faster than usual. At least I don't have to sit in a waiting room, but, my hell, what's the rush? Why is everyone so concerned about swollen glands and a thyroid?*

All she knew was that after months of barely sleeping, she wanted to sleep, which was rare. She wondered how long it would all take. She hoped that maybe they could give her some good drugs and let her go home.

The nurse walked in, handed her a gown, and said, "We're admitting you into the hospital."

Chelsea gasped. "Why? I have barely seen my children in the last two weeks, and I need their hugs."

The nurse smiled and stated, "The doctor will be in shortly. Here are some anti-anxiety drugs to make you more comfortable as you wait."

Chapter 21
A CHANGE BEFORE HER EYES

THE DOCTOR WALKED INTO the room with a long needle and said, "I have to stick this into the lump to draw out the fluid."

Chelsea was as high as a kite and didn't feel anything at all. *I feel all floaty and happy.* She looked over and saw Garrett sitting in the chair next to her bed, bawling like a baby.

When Chelsea was angry, her silent treatment was much better than her words. Even she knew her words were lethal, and she could be downright mean, so she found that not talking was kinder for all parties involved. It was a trait she had learned from her mother.

Well, clearly, these drugs work because the doctor with the long needle isn't even fazing me. Hopefully, when I wake up, I can go home.

BEFORE LONG, SHE WAS wandering through a forest of trees. The trees were all impressively tall and plush. The smell of evergreen and sap instantly made her feel calm and at peace.

In the distance, she could see a path lined with plumerias. She began to walk toward the path, but she was feeling tired, and her eyes were heavy. "I'll lie down for a bit. I'm exhausted, and it isn't like me to be so tired," she whispered as she went to sleep in the meadow beneath the trees.

She didn't know how long she had been asleep but was awakened when she felt something move. It startled her and made her pulse race.

She looked over and saw it was a unicorn. She wiped her eyes to see if she saw it right, but it definitely was a unicorn.

"Well, hello. Come see me," she urged as she approached the unicorn. She touched the unicorn's mane and smiled at the energy she was receiving from it. It made her feel awake and invincible. The unicorn walked beside her as they ventured to the path of plumerias. "I wonder where this path will lead us," she whispered.

"CHELSEA, WAKE UP!"

She felt the nurse shake her.

She abruptly woke from her dream to a nurse standing over her. "You need to stay awake, Chelsea."

"Why?" Chelsea asked.

The nurse smiled and explained, "We have to talk to you about the next steps, and I need you to be awake when the doctor comes back into your room."

Chelsea sighed and rolled her eyes. She was disappointed and wanted to return to her dream. She felt alive and peaceful. *Unicorns are magical, so maybe this whole ER visit is not a big deal.* As the doctor walked into the room.

"Hi, Chelsea," a new doctor said as Garrett sat up straight in his chair. "I'm going to be your oncologist during your treatment."

"Treatment?" Chelsea questioned. "When can I go home?"

"Unfortunately, we need to keep you in the hospital for a couple days. Your condition is quite serious, and the biopsy indicates you have thyroid cancer," he indicated while pulling out a chart to show where the cancer was located. He pointed to the area and stated, "It really is the Cadillac of cancers, because it rarely spreads to the rest of the body. We will have you go to radiation in the morning to kill the thyroid and cancer."

Chelsea sighed. *God must have a sense of humor because this month won't give me a break: marriage, honeymoon, husband screwing friend, annulment, and cancer.*

The doctor continued matter-of-factly. "It was bleeding, and blood was forming into the nodules in your neck. Please rest because you will need surgery after the radiation, and we'll have a surgeon come and talk to you about that in the morning."

Chelsea's mouth was wide open. Most of her family had died from cancer, and two months earlier, her aunt had lost her life to cancer. She was in shock, feeling the tears welling up in her eyes, but she managed to ask, "So, it is curable cancer?"

Garrett's face had a sudden coldness as he said in a shaky voice, "Please excuse me." He then got up out of his chair and left the room, crying.

My good hell! Let's not pick this time to be dramatic, Garrett. I'm clearly not in the mood.

Chelsea asked, "Hey, when he returns, can you tell him that visiting hours are over? He is my estranged husband, and he's the last person I want around for cancer discussions."

"Of course. We can tell him it is time to leave," the nurse said as she touched her arm.

The doctor continued, "It was likely caught fast, but during surgery, we will know if we can get all of it. The thyroid is part of the endocrine system, so you will have to be on medication for the rest of your life. Plus, since you will go from hyperthyroidism to hypothyroidism, your body will go through quite a shock."

Chelsea wanted to know more. "What shock? And the endocrine system? Like Diabetes?"

The doctor looked impressed that she at least knew what the endocrine system was and said, "Yes, like diabetes, but you will have radiation, surgery, and then more radiation again. Since the thyroid changes your body, it is not an easy process." He then paused as Garrett walked back into the room.

"Garrett, the rest of this consultation is for the patient only. We will need to excuse you for another time," the nurse said politely as she took his arm and led him out of the room.

Garrett looked shocked but said over his shoulder, "I'll still be here for you, and I love you, Chels."

The doctor waited for Garrett to leave and then continued. "An endocrinologist can tell you the specifics. I recommend seeing him regularly after the surgery. Hyperthyroidism likely made you hot all the time, faint, have headaches, heart palpitations, trouble sleeping, losing weight, etcetera."

"Oh, my goodness! That's why I was dropping weight like crazy, and I ate constantly. What will happen after surgery?"

The doctor smiled and said, "You will go through being cold, gaining weight, depression, feeling sleepy all the time, feeling unmotivated, and you'll have some headaches. I recommend patients start with depression medication and thyroid medication immediately so the crash won't feel as bad, but there will be a crash."

Chelsea looked at him and stated, "Well, let's get that prescription going!"

Chapter 22
SILENCE YOUR PHONE

———

ONCE SHE WAS ON the table in the operating room, the anesthesiologist asked if she was ready to begin. She told him, yes, and he injected something into Chelsea's IV.

"Time to count backward," he told her.

"Ten, nine, eight…."

She was asleep.

CHELSEA FELT FLOATY AND yet very happy. In the distance, she saw the waterfall, the field, and the plumerias. She walked into them and could feel them tickle her feet, and with each step, she could smell their aroma.

She could hear children playing in the background. She wanted to go join them—she could use more play in her life. She started toward the sound of the children when a sudden onset of panic arose. What if she was dead? She instantly felt scared to go see them and sat on the park bench instead. A woman came and sat beside her, her Aunt Nancy, who had recently lost her battle with breast cancer. "Hi, Chels!" she exclaimed with a big smile.

"Nancy! I have missed you so much. I never got to say goodbye," she exclaimed as she gave her a long hug. Chelsea asked, "Wait, am I dying—or dead?"

Nancy smiled at Chelsea, glanced at the children, and said, "It'll all be alright! It is not your time yet." She touched her hand, which sent chills through Chelsea.

"I love you! He loves you!" Nancy declared as she turned into a bright light, like a firefly, and floated away.

Chelsea realized that she needed to change who she had become. She needed to change how she has lived. There was no doubt in her mind that God loved her, but she knew that she needed to be an example of love, inspiration and positivity. Somehow she knew that would be her life's purpose and legacy.

"CHELSEA," SHE COULD FEEL someone shaking her and saying her name. It was the nurse. "You need to take deep breaths and try to wake up now. You are not breathing."

Chelsea was exhausted. She wanted to go back to her dream and learn what else she needed to do. She could hear herself breathing, so what was the nurse talking about? She tried to say the words out loud, but they wouldn't come out.

She opened her eyes and saw her entire family—plus Jessica, Freddy, Garrett, and Freddy's family—in the room. She definitely wanted to go back to sleep now, especially because half of the group were people she didn't want to see. She felt like she had left heaven to be tossed into hell.

"I barely had surgery and want to sleep. My family is fine to stay and Jessica, but everyone else needs to go," she whispered to the nurse.

The nurse tactfully said in a booming voice, "I'm sorry, but only two visitors at a time, please."

Her dad, mom, and sister grabbed her hands and squeezed them gently as they exited. Freddy touched her foot, and Garrett kissed her on the forehead before leaving.

"Chelsea, your throat is healing, so you need to try not to talk for the next few hours and, if possible, a few days. If you need more painkillers, push this button," the nurse exclaimed.

"What can I do for you?" Jessica asked.

Chelsea smiled under her oxygen mask. "Get me a pen and paper, so I don't have to talk."

Jessica grabbed a pen and paper from her purse and gave them to Chelsea.

Chelsea wrote *I love you! Now go home to your fiancé.*

Jessica smiled, nodded, and walked out of the room, saying, "I'll see you soon."

Chelsea pushed the painkiller button and prayed, "Please let me return to the peace and happiness I felt with my Aunt Nancy. I wasn't taught what was next, and my throat hurts so bad right now."

Two days later was discharge day, and Chelsea could hardly wait to leave the hospital. She was finally going to be able to see her children before the last radiation treatment. Plus, she'd finally be able to sleep without nurses interrupting her slumber.

She arrived home to find her mom there with the kids. She immediately rushed over to them and began to hug and kiss them.

Mace kept trying to touch her neck, saying, "Ouch. What happened?"

Chelsea smiled at him. "I have a boo-boo, but it's almost all better."

She only had a couple of days, and she wanted to make the best of them. It was difficult, however, because she could barely move, and simple things like changing a diaper wiped her out. She was working from home and trying to function with her children, which resulted in not getting much work done.

A WEEK LATER, SHE packed a few things for her radiation the next day. She could barely sleep because she knew that after she dropped the children off at her parents' house, it was going to be another five long days without them. She dreaded the quiet, lonely home.

Garrett came to pick her up, as they had agreed, for the last day of her treatment.

The whole ride was awkward, and she wondered why she had agreed to let him take her in the first place.

She closed her eyes and leaned up against the window. She could feel Garrett looking at her, but she was lost in her thoughts.

He shook her shoulder to wake her up just as she had barely fallen asleep. He stated, "Babe, I think this is a good time for us to talk. Can you stay awake, please?"

I can barely talk, and he decides that now is an excellent time to talk.

She snapped, "Garrett! Can you please stop? I have plenty going on right now, and I can't take this. You demanded to take me to radiation. I'm letting you take me to ease your conscience, but I'm not going to hear you ramble false apologies," Chelsea said calmly in her hoarse voice. "You cheated. It's over. Want to be friends? Then be a friend."

Garrett looked at her and then back at the road. "I'm sorry, and yes, you're right. I love you, and I'll let you deal with this for a while. It was my fault that I added even more stress to you. I hoped we could talk today about maybe making up."

Chelsea stared out the window and let her silence be her reply.

They arrived at the hospital and went to the radiation therapy area. Chelsea changed into a gown while Garrett was in the waiting room, receiving instructions for Chelsea's post-care.

"Chelsea, we have one more patient ahead of you, so we won't move you to the waiting room until we are ready," the nurse explained.

Garrett entered, and they both sat in the small room, silently waiting until Garrett's phone began to ring. It kept ringing to the point that Chelsea was annoyed, wondering why he would keep the phone ringing instead of silencing it.

After the third time, she had to say something. "Is it work? I'm a couple hours out if you need to go work from the lobby."

Garrett nodded, kissed her on the forehead even though she was turning away from him and walked out. When he left, she was relieved. The stress and tension of him around made her sicker. She felt like she could see orbs forming in the back of her head, and feel a migraine coming on.

By now, she had learned that migraines were her body's way of letting her know that someone was toxic. Almost as though, her intuition was screaming for her to run away from someone.

The nurse came in, and Chelsea informed her, "I think I have anxiety or stress from all of this. Is it okay if I go back to my locker and grab a migraine pill? I have the orbs and dots thing happening in front of my eyes, and if I don't take a pill now, it will seem like I am having a stroke."

"Oh, yes, the radiation can be done regardless of what is in your system. Come right back, and we will take you in," the nurse said empathetically.

Chelsea grabbed the pills, taking them dry before returning to the waiting room.

The nurse smiled and asked, "Are you ready for the second rendition of the space show?"

An inside joke had formed between the two of them after Chelsea's last treatment. She reminisced her shock when she felt like she had been transported to space. She was put into an all-white room with a silver machine in the middle. The door was behind two other doors. In the room, there was a glass window similar to that of a box office with a small opening at the bottom. A man showed up in a shiny space suit and used a metal arm to administer medication through the tiny glass window. She couldn't believe that she was being told to take the medicine that nobody dared touch or breathe.

Chelsea gave a whispered laugh before quietly responding, "Let's go get our space on."

AFTER THE RADIATION, SHE sat in the recovery room for two hours.

Garrett was nowhere in sight.

She called him, but there was no answer. She dressed and told the nurses that he must be working from the lobby, and she was alright to check herself out.

After another hour, without any response from him and several unsuccessful hospital-wide pages, she called him once more and left a voicemail.

"Seriously, Garrett, where the hell are you? Why did you beg me to let you take me to radiation if you knew that you were going to be unavailable? My neck hurts, my head hurts, and I feel dazed. Get back here, ASAP," she hissed with her hoarse voice.

She went back to the lobby and stood by the door, looking out the glass panes for his Jeep. Suddenly, everything went black, and she collapsed.

"HI, CHELSEA," SHE HEARD as she was waking up. It was her nurse friend from radiation. She looked around to see that she was back on a gurney wearing an oxygen mask, "Sorry, honey. We cannot release you until someone comes to get you now. We contacted your husband to make sure that he was coming back, and he's on his way."

"What time is it?" Chelsea asked weakly.

The nurse looked above Chelsea, spotting a clock on the wall and replied, "It is 4 P.M."

Chelsea felt her blood boil. She had been in the hospital for five hours, and Garrett left more than four and a half hours earlier.

He was the one that begged me to let him take me to radiation, and he is not even here.

ANOTHER HOUR WENT BY before Garrett arrived, and during that time, the nurse became more and more agitated by his delay. "Would you like me to call someone else?" she asked.

Chelsea was ready to agree when Garrett came running into the lobby. He told the nurse, "My Jeep is parked out front."

The nurse and Chelsea nodded. Chelsea saw that the nurse's expression was the same pissed-off look that Chelsea was giving. Chelsea was put in a wheelchair, escorted to the Jeep, and helped up into the passenger seat while Garrett hopped into the driver's seat.

As he was driving her home, he kept apologizing, "I'm so sorry! I had to run into work for an issue and didn't think it would take that long."

Chelsea could only nod her head as she felt her migraine coming back. She could see that Garrett had a smear of lipstick on his cheek, and he reeked of Monica's cheap perfume.

"Can you drive faster, please? I don't feel good and want to go home," she asked, ignoring his pointless and false apologies.

Apologizing without the necessary actions is manipulation. I should've asked Jessica to pick me up.

"Babe! Are you okay? You look really pale," Garrett asked, pausing from droning on with his pointless babbling.

The migraines made her uncontrollably ill. Sometimes they were so bad they left her looking like a stroke victim with half of her face completely numb.

Chelsea asked, "Please pull over."

Garrett barely came to a stop on the roadside before she began throwing up stomach acid over and over.

It's official. After today I will never speak to Garrett again. She returned to the Jeep.

"Babe! Are you okay?" Garrett asked.

Chelsea said nothing for a few minutes before finally nodding. "Please, no more words. Just get me home." They arrived at the house that once was their home.

"Can I come in?" he asked.

She looked at him, deadpanned. "I already asked for no more words. I'm home. Thank you for making this all so easy."

She jumped out and slammed the door to his Jeep as hard as she could. She went straight to her medicine cabinet and took two more migraine pills.

Chapter 23
DEPRESSION CANNOT HIT A MOVING TARGET

"TODAY I MADE IT without shedding a single tear until noon," Chelsea wrote in her journal, a slight smile forming on her lips. She found that it was hard to even brush her teeth each day, and she started to write down small accomplishments when she had them.

If they bring you peace when they are no longer around, then it isn't actually losing them.

Of course, she was still her responsible and upbeat self in front of others, but behind closed doors, she was a vulnerable twenty-three-year-old who was fighting for her will to live.

She didn't attempt suicide, but she had many thoughts about suicide—she knew she could never do that to her family or her children. She found that the struggle to actually live life and not remain in bed was an uphill battle every day.

Each morning, she put on a fake smile and pretended that life was happy in front of everyone. She was so masterful at the task that she internally laughed sarcastically when a coworker told her how brilliant, outgoing, and full of life she was.

The doctor had warned her that these feelings would be normal post-surgery, but she felt like it was more than a missing gland. Life was not as she had planned, and instead of getting better, it seemed to be continuously getting worse. Her hopes and dreams were continually shattered; she had been betrayed by those she loved.

The doctor had prescribed more drugs for her to take and scheduled another follow-up visit a month after the surgery. This became her routine. Meet the doctor, describe her depression, up her meds, or change them, reschedule. Meet the doctor, express sadness, up her meds, or change them, reschedule, rinse, repeat.

Chelsea didn't realize it, but day by day, she was getting better. She kept thinking about her children, and that reminded her of all that she had to live for. She thought about her job and how much she liked it. Weeks went by, and one day, she noticed that she was singing along to the songs on the radio.

"I haven't cried for a week," she realized as she spoke to herself in the car.

When she arrived home, she realized how different everything seemed. It didn't seem like an impossible task to make dinner, change diapers, or put the kids in the bath. Okay, the tub was still an undertaking, but as Tabby poured water from her play cup out of the bathtub and onto the floor, Chelsea was actually able to smile and say, "Well, at least the bathroom floor gets cleaned daily."

After the children fell asleep, she decided to start a new ritual of writing three things she was thankful for, and then three things she would strive to accomplish the next day in her journal. As she put the journal away and began getting ready for bed, she found herself smiling in the mirror.

You've got this, Chels, she told herself.

Chapter 24
MY RELIGION IS LOVE

THINGS KEPT IMPROVING FOR Chelsea. Her recovery went well, and Mace finally exited the diaper stage. And overall, the drama in her life was slim.

Moreover, Chelsea was making friends all over the neighborhood. One, in particular, Laurie, became an instant bestie. She started to bring her daughter over almost every night to play, and she and Chelsea would talk nonstop about their days.

Tabby and Laurie's daughter, Patty, were practically inseparable. They dressed alike, they played with the same types of toys, and they both loved cheerleading and dance.

Chelsea felt like she didn't always have to be worried that Tabby would bully Patty, which was a rare thing, but it was because Patty had enough spunk herself that she could put eight-year-old Tabby back in line if she needed to.

Tabby was always in trouble at school and at home, much to Chelsea's dismay. Tabby didn't have many friends.

Clearly, she got her mood swings and bratty behavior from Freddy, Chelsea would think to herself.

It was hard to have the resident mean kid with no idea how to stop it. Chelsea tried everything—she gave Tabby more attention, then less, then more. She took her to get pedicures, to movies, to help at charities, and played dress-up with her, but Tabby had an odd and evil side to her that nothing could quell. It was as though Tabby was even jealous of her own mother.

Mace was the opposite. He was the calm, sweet, and loving child that everyone wanted to watch and be around. He was even kind to Tabby, who would frequently punch him or bite him for no reason.

ONE DAY AFTER SCHOOL, Tabby came in and declared, "Patty is baptized, and I want to be baptized like her."

Chelsea guided her to sit down and asked, "Well, what do you know about religion?"

"Who cares? You go to church, and then you won't have any more sins. They are gone when you are baptized," Tabby said as matter-of-factly.

Chelsea tilted her head and tried to gently correct her. "Did you know that I was baptized when I was eight years old? But I only attended church three times for funerals, and that was it. I made a huge commitment to a church that I never understood because all of my friends were baptized."

Tabby sassed her back. "Well, you have to go to church, mom!"

"You are right. You do have to go to church. You also have to do as you are asked and be loving to others," Chelsea replied back. "Are you ready to go to church and be loving to others?"

"Yes. DUH!" Tabby said.

Chelsea tried to ignore the fact that Tabby was becoming rude and smiled. "Well, I'll tell you what. We will go to church every single Sunday, and then, after six months, you can make the call to be baptized or not. Okay?"

Tabby roared, "Okay!"

Maybe church and the fear of God will snap the brat right out of her.

Tabby stood up to run toward her room, pushing Mace out of her way, so he fell back onto the couch. Chelsea sighed, *I can't wait until the day she has a child like her.*

Chelsea yelled, "Tabby, get back here. Now! And apologize."

OVER THE NEXT SEVERAL months, Chelsea kept her word and made sure that she, Mace, and Tabby were in attendance at the local church every single Sunday.

The rest of Chelsea's family even started to attend the church, and she'd be lying if she said there was no effect.

Chelsea saw that her dad had more patience and wanted to see her children more. Chelsea had always had a weird relationship with him growing up. She, like most daughters, adored him, but she still felt like nothing ever seemed good enough in his eyes. Somehow, though, his attendance in the church was changing him. He was more accepting and more verbally complimentary.

A few years earlier, right before Chelsea's cancer, she had lost a lot of respect for her dad by watching the way he treated her mom. They were still married, but he treated her as a servant and didn't show her the affection she deserved. Around that same time, she found out that he had a four-year affair when Chelsea had been a teenager. It crushed her heart, knowing her own dad could do that to her mom, but when it happened to Chelsea, the wound was reopened.

Now, though, things felt a bit different. This new version of her dad seemed forgivable, and Chelsea liked seeing her family bond, even if she wasn't sure why this bonding had to have a religious aspect behind it. Chelsea was desperate and willing to do anything that would help her with Tabby, even if it meant religion.

Tabby was eventually baptized, and after that, Chelsea started to receive quite a few "callings," invitations to perform some duty in the church. Chelsea felt like these callings were an equal exchange, given the way Tabby was behaving. Tabby was improving simply by attending weekly, and she felt like she was finally surrounded by loyal people who genuinely cared about her and her family.

At work, everyone loved hearing how Chelsea had found religion, and they often asked her questions about what she thought of her callings.

She never said it to her churchmates, but Chelsea still felt it seemed like some kind of cult, only it was with sweet and supportive people who cared about her instead of the crazy poison-drinking kind. Chelsea didn't feel like her attendance at church was helping her find God. She felt like she already had a very personal relationship with him on her own because, to her, God was love, and she had lots of love with her friends and family. Love had always been her religion. She did enjoy the social aspect of attending church, though, and again, it was a fair trade for the help with Tabby.

One of her employees, Kara, was an active attendee of the singles wards at the church, and she often pleaded with Chelsea to participate with her.

After weeks of pushing, Chelsea reluctantly agreed, but as she entered the chapel, she felt like a fish out of water, watching everyone looked her up and down.

Kara giggled as she stated, "Look at you, the new fresh meat."

Chelsea chuckled and replied, "Do I have an A on my fore-head, and they think I am Jezebel? The women are giving me evil glares, and the men are making me feel like I'm naked in church."

"It is because you are gorgeous, Chels," Kara declared. "Ignore the jealous women."

Chelsea sighed. "Well, I am not in a competition, and I'm certainly not here to date. So they all can relax. Maybe I should put that on my forehead."

Kara laughed as she pulled Chelsea toward Aaron, sitting in the back row. Aaron would often come by work to join them for lunch because his brother worked with them both.

Although Aaron was handsome in a boy-next-door type of way, Chelsea wasn't sure about him. He seemed a little shy with his tight and rigid posture. Yet he wasn't stand-offish—he remained friendly—and his body posture was welcoming, and his cheeks became rosy when he talked to her. She thought he was sincere, but she didn't know if she could trust her instincts anymore.

Garrett had seemed like a gentleman, too, and she knew how that turned out.

She was finally back into a functional space and happy. And she was busy, too. Way too busy for another man to take up more of her time.

She had recently enrolled in college, was attending church, and had church callings, a full-time job, lots of overtime, two children, and, well, the life of a single mom. She didn't mind her career and would take classes online as the kids were asleep next to her. It's not like she needed a man. Besides, her goal was to finish college and be the first person in her family to graduate.

Although she could admit that Aaron did seem terrific, she wasn't really interested in having a man enter her life again. She had explained that to Aaron, but he still would try by sending Chelsea random texts throughout her day, bringing her treats or food, and asking her out on dates. She graciously declined any advances made by him or others.

Why is he so interested in me? Aren't there plenty of other, more churchy-type girls? she wondered.

Later that night, she decided she was not going to go back to the singles' ward and called Kara to apologize.

"I'm sorry, Kara. I feel like a piece of meat, and I'm way too busy. Plus, who would want a divorcé, with two babies anyways? I am twenty-seven years old and not married, which, in this weird Utah culture, is considered an old maid. I think I'd rather focus on what I already have on my plate and be alone with my kids," she explained as she rejected Kara's offer to join her the following Sunday.

"I understand, Chelsea, but are you sure?" Kara asked.

"I'm so sure. I finally feel like things are going in the right direction at work, school, church, friends, finances, promotions, and children. The thought of going to a ward where people just want to date one another seems way out of my comfort zone," Chelsea chuckled.

Chelsea did want a happy married life, but she also had resigned herself to the burden of being a single mother forever. "I have no desire to find a man," she asserted. It was a lie, but she corrected it by stating, "If the universe wants me to have one, it can align it all for me."

OVER THE NEXT SEVERAL months, she dove into her career and schooling, but it seemed like everywhere she went, Aaron would happen to be there. He would come to her work, which was understandable because his younger brother worked there, but she also saw him at social gatherings, church meetings, and even the grocery store.

She found it odd that after meeting him, he was everywhere, and she thought he might be stalking her, but then one time she showed up at a party after him. So maybe the world had become a bit smaller, or he was like a new word you learn, and then you start hearing everywhere—or maybe this was the universe making things align

It was tax season, and it felt like everyone was losing their minds. Chelsea and her team worked overtime to help customers because the whole system had decided to shut down, making everyone suddenly swamped.

After seven hours without a break, she looked over by the printer on her desk and saw a lunch box, a cookie, and a note that said *Hard day? Talk to customers in between bites. I was thinking about you. – Aaron.*

Food on an empty stomach was one flirty advancement she couldn't ignore. She followed Aaron's instructions and took tiny bites between phone calls, which allowed her to respond without sounding rude and eating on the phone.

After thirteen hours, the day was over, and the system was finally working again. Chelsea sent a canned message for her staff to submit to customers.

An hour later, she was able to shut down the phone lines and lock up the building. It was not unusual for Chelsea to lock up the building at night and work longer than anyone else. She had to cross everything off her list before she could actually sit down and relax. Her work ethic came with a price for everyone who knew her, mainly her children, while she worked overtime.

"Well, if the worst thing I do is work hard to provide for them, then they don't have it too hard. The kids could be living on the streets, which is what would have happened if they lived with Freddy," she told herself as she drove home.

One thing she did know was that her children were being catered to and absolutely spoiled by her family during tax season. They were even taken to Disneyland and never had to go without anything they might need.

She knew how blessed she was to have such a supportive family that helped her as much as they did. It definitely eased the burden of feeling all the weight on her own shoulders. Plus, her hard work was being appreciated, and she was being promoted and given raises any time the company could. Sometimes, to thank her, the company would give her a massage package or something else to indicate that her efforts didn't go unnoticed.

After a long night, she arrived home, and her mom was there with the children already in bed.

"Mom, thank you so much. It has been a hell of a day," Chelsea sighed.

Her mom smiled. "I ironed all the clothes and put them away. I saw a few holes in socks, so I fixed those and also put food in the fridge for you."

Chelsea started crying. Her mom knew it was tears of gratitude.

"Get some rest, and the next day like this, I can keep them overnight, okay?" her mom said. Chelsea nodded her head and started heating up the food.

Once her mom left, she ate her dinner in the bathtub. She tried to occupy every moment of free time efficiently, but she couldn't enjoy much of anything entirely, either.

Chapter 25
A PICNIC IN THE PARK

"**D**ID AARON LEAVE LUNCH for you yesterday so that you were able to eat?" Chelsea asked.

"No," Kara replied and walked off, giving Chelsea a look.

Tax season was taking a toll on everyone, but Kara was new to tax season. Maybe she was tired and going through a hard time. If she was moody and snapping after tax season, Chelsea was sure she would tell her if something was wrong.

Chelsea tried again to engage her. "Kara, if you remember, I have to go to the doctor on Wednesday. Are you okay covering for me?" Chelsea asked.

"Yes! I already said I would last month when you asked," Kara snapped.

"Thanks," Chelsea said as she walked off, *something is wrong here.*

A WEEK LATER, CHELSEA was training Kara on a new program.

Chelsea's phone started ringing, and she looked down. "Oh, it's the doctor, let me get this," Chelsea exclaimed as she watched Kara roll her eyes. Kara sat there, listening to the one-sided conversation.

"Ms. Hansen, can you come in for an appointment to discuss your results?" the doctor asked.

Chelsea replied, "Can I get them over the phone? I'm extremely busy at work?"

"I hate to inform you, but you have precancerous cells in your cervix," the doctor stated.

"Okay, when do you want me to come back in?" Chelsea said into the phone. She turned to Kara. "Kara, you will have to excuse me. I need to take a break," Chelsea said as she walked out the door, not waiting for a response.

After a few minutes of tears, she wiped them away and collected herself. "Oh my hell, Chels, stop being a boob. You are fine. Go back to work," she told herself, looking in the rearview mirror of her car.

She walked back into the office, still upset, and went over to Kara. "I need to leave tomorrow for an appointment for problems in my cervix," Chelsea sighed, feeling broken and looking for support from her friend and coworker.

Kara looked blankly at the screen in front of her and shook her head, barely acknowledging Chelsea.

"What is going on with you? Do you have anything to say other than one-word answers or nothing at all?" Chelsea snapped.

"I am fine!" Kara exclaimed, pushing away from the desk and storming off. *Clearly, she must be going through something.*

MONTHS WENT BY, AND one night, Aaron stopped by her home unannounced. "Um, hi Aaron, come in," she said, wondering what he wanted, but felt it would be rude to ask that.

He played with the children, and they chatted, and then he left. After a couple weeks, the same thing happened a few more times, and he started to do other little, thoughtful things for Chelsea. Finally, he asked, "Chels, will you go out with me?"

"Um. Yes. When and what do you have in mind? You know my schedule," she replied.

AARON SAT ENGROSSED, BARELY noticing the popcorn falling into his lap as he put his arm around Chelsea. She could tell his focus was scattered, but he was also filled with nervous anticipation. At first, Chelsea felt herself tighten out of fear, but then, as she felt his sweet touch caressing her shoulders, she relaxed. She looked over, and his eyes met hers, and they shared a smile. She felt her face flush as she gently grabbed his knee.

Throughout the movie, they were both smiling. Chelsea could feel a tingling feeling spread throughout her entire body as he pulled her closer. *I can feel his heartbeat slowly accelerating.*

As they arrived at Chelsea's house. They sat in the car with the sunroof open, looking at the stars. They didn't speak, because in their own way they were already communicating.

Aaron walked Chelsea to the door. She threw her arms over his shoulders as he pulled her in closer. She felt a fire ignite as his face came closer to hers. He waited, not daring to kiss her. She leaned in, opened her mouth slightly, and they kissed repeatedly.

She went into the house, then closed the door and leaned against it. Her body felt like it was in a trance. She felt invincible and had such a wide grin that she worried about her cheeks splitting open.

Chelsea turned on the music to calm her soul. Suddenly every love song she heard was about Aaron.

CHELSEA FELT A PHYSICAL and emotional connection to Aaron. She trusted him with her raw feelings like their souls had been spiritually connected. She wondered if their souls had met in a previous life, like the strings of fate were intertwining in them. She wasn't sure, but she knew she had fallen in love again, a phenomenon she thought would never happen. Chelsea met Jessica for dinner to catch up with Jessica's marriage and to talk about Aaron.

Chelsea swooned to Jessica as she talked about how she and Aaron went river rafting with a church group. "Aaron led the trip. He was charismatic as he spoke to the masses . . . and soft as he introduced me. He beams when he says my name. It made me melt.

Jessica smiled as she gushed, "Sounds like someone is twitterpatted. Even though I feel like the church is a cult, it is nice to see you happy with a good man."

Chelsea giggled. "It is nice to see us both with good men."

Chelsea continued to tell Jessica how Aaron romanced Chelsea with candlelit, home-cooked dinners. And how he brought her plumerias to surprise her at work. Chelsea went on and on about how Aaron even spoiled her children with games, toys, and fun outings.

Jessica grinned wide. "He is hot and romantic. You go, girl."

Chelsea blushed as she said, "I think he is the one, Jess. I really do."

WEEKS LATER, AARON CAME over to watch TV and help put the children to bed, a nightly routine they had been doing for weeks. Chelsea noticed Aaron's posture was stand-offish, and he was communicating in one-word statements. *Oh, boy! He is in a mood. I'll go put the children to bed, and hopefully, he'll snap out of it because I'm not in the mood for him to be in a mood.*

She came downstairs and sighed. "Do you need water or anything?"

Aaron looked at her. "We need to talk."

Chelsea looked at him and asked, "Okay. What's on your mind?"

"I am falling in love with you," Aaron said.

Chelsea chimed in and said, "I feel the same way."

He put his hand up and continued. "I can't have someone else's children and don't want to date you anymore."

Chelsea felt like she had been punched in the stomach. "You pursued me, you came into our lives, you knew that I had children and how I felt about them from the beginning. You knew I was a package deal, and I didn't even want a man in my life, but you were relentless."

She stood up and pointed to the door. He started to say something but held his words and walked out the door. Chelsea stepped up the stairs. She could hold her heartbreak no longer as she fell to the floor in a disheveled heap as her grief and disbelieve poured out into uncontrollable tears.

A MONTH LATER, CHELSEA heard a rapid knocking on her door. She swung it open to see Aaron standing there at her door, looking manic. Without a word, he walked into her home uninvited and then began talking.

"Um, Aaron now is not a good time," Chelsea stammered as he turned into the living room and found Laurie with the kids playing on the floor.

He looked shocked. "Hi, I'm Aaron."

Laurie gave an awkward smile. "Yeah, I know." But her look said, *what in the hell are you doing here?*

Aaron stayed there in the hall, not understanding that he was interrupting the friendly get-together.

Finally, Chelsea said, "You know, Aaron, now isn't a good time. Can we have a conversation later?"

Aaron looked at her a little surprised, as though he had been lost in thought, and she was his lifeline. "What about tomorrow night?"

Chelsea looked at him before sucking in her breath. "Sure, that's fine. Or you can call," she said as she made a sweeping motion toward the door.

She really didn't want to discuss anything with him but was willing to agree to anything to get him to leave her house. In her eyes, their previous discussion had made things clear and entirely over.

"I certainly don't need him to be my friend, to ease his mind," she later told Laurie.

CHELSEA'S STOMACH ACHED AS she waited for Aaron to show up at her house that night. She didn't want to deal with the drama or even talk to Aaron, but she, too, had things to say to him, particularly about using her kids as the excuse to break up.

The kids were with her mother, and she wondered how long this conversation would last.

She heard a knock on the door.

Chelsea opened the door and didn't say a word, but she motioned for Aaron to come in. Aaron walked in with his head down and shoulders hunched. Chelsea noticed that his blue eyes were droopy and swollen.

Aaron sat down, and Chelsea continued to stand, indicating, not so subtly, that she didn't want him to get comfortable. Aaron motioned for her to sit down, so she rolled her eyes and sat down.

"I made a rash decision and found myself only missing you, Tabby, and Mace. I know you're a package deal. You are always upfront and honest. I promise if you give me another chance that I will not let you down, and I will love the children like they're my own," Aaron stammered as he began apologizing profusely.

Chelsea sat there, dumbfounded. "Well, I don't know if I like you anymore. Come give me a kiss, and I'll see."

Aaron leaned in, and their fantastic make-up kiss kept going until they heard the garage door go up. It was her mom bringing the kids back from seeing their cousins.

Tabby bounced in and sat on Aaron's lap. Mace plopped himself on the couch, grabbed the remote, and then turned on the TV.

It was as though he never left.

WEEKS PASSED, AND AARON and Chelsea spent almost every night and every weekend together with the children. They went to church, and Chelsea did a spiritual advancement, called her endowments, with Aaron present. The only time the two of them didn't spend together anymore was lunch.

One day, out of the blue, Aaron showed up as Chelsea was working and stated, "I'm taking you to lunch."

Chelsea giggled. "Okay, let me get someone to cover me."

She started walking down the hall and saw Kara.

"Hey, can you cover for me while I go to lunch today? When I get back, you can either leave early or take a longer lunch," Chelsea pleaded.

Kara gave a half-smile. "Okay."

Chelsea walked back into her office and said to Aaron, "Let's go! Kara is covering, but she's been back in her snippy mood so, I can't be gone long."

Aaron drove them both to a tiny park. A slight breeze rustled the leaves that fell into the mossy pond where a family of ducks frolicked in the pond. Old trees bordered the lush, green hills, muffling the sound of the busy city all around.

Chelsea exclaimed, "Aw, this is the same park we met at."

He smiled as he was putting down a blanket and a picnic box full of food and declared, "Is it?" His tone implied he already knew which park it was.

They ate, talked, and laughed.

Aaron wrapped Chelsea close into his arm. She rested her head upon his chest as if all worries were hugged away. She was naming cloud shapes and saw one that looked like a plumeria.

"Hey, look at that. It is a plumeria. A special sign," she told him as she pointed it out.

He smiled and sat up, looking adoringly at her. "Speaking of rare but amazing flowers—" He got down on one knee, pulled a ring box out from his pocket, opened it, and declared, "Chels, you mean the world to me, and so do the children. There is nobody on earth I would rather spend the rest of my life with than you. Will you marry me?"

Chelsea's eyes went wide. She stood up and pulled him up to join her, kissing him. "Of course, I will!"

"Good thing. I already booked the temple. It is in three months," Aaron stated.

They went back to the office soon after that, and Chelsea couldn't wait to tell Kara. She walked in and ran up to Kara. "Guess what?"

She showed her ring finger to Kara. Kara seemed to swallow hard before saying, in a meek voice, "Cool."

Chelsea looked at her, confused, and a little taken aback. She walked out of her office when she realized that was all Kara was going to say.

Chelsea immediately called Jessica to tell her all about it. As they were talking, an email came in from Kara.

It was a resignation letter.

CHELSEA WAS NERVOUS ABOUT getting married again. Aaron was everything she wanted in a man—honest, trustworthy, respectable, kind, smart, handsome, loved the children—but she couldn't shake the feeling in the bottom of her stomach that something was going to go wrong.

I guess this is what having cold feet means.

She pushed through and arrived at her church's temple. She was immediately ushered through a unique set of doors into a "sacred place."

Before going into the ceremony room, she was given a different name, a name given to her that only Aaron would know.

It was things like this that made her feel like she was in a cult.

She wondered what would happen if she started to run out of the room. Would the elderly church servants catch her and tackle her for going into a forbidden room? What if they sacrificed a virgin or animal during the ceremony, and she didn't know it would happen until she was there?

She was so lost in thought that she almost missed Aaron's speech as he exclaimed, "Oh my, Chelsea! The name the church gave you is the same name that I was told in prayer that I would marry one day, Rachel."

This caused Chelsea to pause. "Isn't Rachel the name of your ex-girlfriend? Don't you think maybe that is why it came to you in prayer?"

Aaron laughed at her comment as though it was a hilarious joke. "For a spiritual person, you sure do question everything. It was before I met her, and that is why I was so torn up when the two of us broke up because I thought she was my forever spouse.

Turns out that you are mine forever. I have never felt surer of that than today."

Aaron gushed as he held her hand.

The ceremony room was peaceful and serene as they both said their vows for eternity. Then, they exchanged rings as a symbol of their promises.

Oh, thank God we are not sacrificing an animal or virgin.

SHE WALKED OUT OF the temple holding Aaron's hand and was immediately welcomed by Jessica and her family. They had to wait outside of the temple, because they weren't part of a particular group in the church, much to Chelsea's displeasure.

As they were taking photos and videos, Chelsea felt a migraine coming on. She pulled Jessica aside. "Please tell me that you have some migraine pills with you."

"I sure do. Orb stage now?" Jessica asked, reaching into her purse.

"Yes, so if I catch it now, it will just be a dull headache," Chelsea said, taking the pills that Jessica handed her and began chewing them up. The taste was disgusting, but soon the pain faded into a dull ache that she could deal with while they finished up.

They wrapped everything up at the temple. Chelsea felt relieved that her swirl of sickening fears disappeared. She was finally married to an amazing man who loved her. She always felt worthy of long-lasting love, but she never thought she would find it after Garrett. As Chelsea was lost in her thoughts, Aaron walked over to her and moved the hair from her eyes.

She felt her face soften as he kissed her and declared, "I am the happiest man on the planet. You are everything I have ever wanted."

The reception, like the rest of the wedding, was beautiful. Chelsea had to admit that they made an adorable couple. Afterward, they jumped into the car and drove to a themed resort for the night. Chelsea was surprisingly nervous about having sex again. As part of her vows to the church, she had given up having sex, and it had been years. She felt comforted by the fact that Aaron was probably as nervous since he was still a virgin.

When they arrived, the anxiety soon passed for both of them as she came out of the bathroom wearing a red lace cutout bra, panties with a matching garter belt and thigh high stockings. He immediately walked towards the bathroom and lifted her right off her feet. He carried her towards the bed and let her fall with a soft bounce on the mattress. They locked eyes for a moment as they started to kiss. After several minutes of kissing, she rolled him over, straddling him, and took off her bra. She grabbed his heads and placed them on her breasts as a small but teasing smile crept on her face. She reached for his underwear and slid it off. She caressed his penis ever so gently and ran her fingers up his chest. She began kissing him again as she slid him inside of her. They both let out a moan as they moved with raw intensity and passion.

Chapter 26
FORGET FOLLOWING MY LEADERS

CHELSEA WALKED DOWN A trail with Aaron, pushing a stroller. The sky was a turquoise blue with wispy looking clouds. She looked up and noticed an oddly shaped cloud in the distance. It was a big and round balloon. It floated left and right and then up and down. She stopped walking and pointed it out to Aaron, but he couldn't find it. Suddenly it burst, and an angel floated out of it.

Chelsea exclaimed, "Aaron, look, do you see it now with the angel?" Aaron shook his head.

She found it odd that she was the only one that could see the balloon or the angel. The angel began to float down to them. The angel was not reflecting the sunlight but emitting it and glowing from within. His skin was translucent with bronze and metallic shimmer to it.

He paused and spoke in a deep voice, "Protect and love that baby." He pointed to the stroller.

Chelsea lifted up the blanket to see a perfect baby boy with porcelain skin.

She shook her head and said, "We will take care of him."

Aaron looked puzzled and said to Chelsea, "What are you talking about?"

She looked appalled. "I'm answering the angel about the baby."

Aaron began to walk off as he sighed, "There is no angel, there is no baby, and there is no balloon in the sky. What does that all mean?"

She chuckled, "Why is it you can't see it and you are the one that is supposed to lead our family to God?"

Aaron rolled his eyes as he continued to walk on.

The angel spoke, "You are blessed to see and know things that others don't. Don't mind him at all and know you are going to be rewarded with an angel for yourself."

BEEP! BEEP! BEEP! CHELSEA looked at the clock and sighed. She had taken time off of work to have another surgery to remove the cancerous cells in her cervix that day.

After her dream and several other occasions, she had serious doubts about the church and decided to make an appointment with her bishop to ask him her questions in person.

A couple days later, she met him. They exchanged a few pleasantries and then she began. "I don't get a few things, and I would like to go over my list. I feel like the church claims to be all about family, but the actions do not reflect that. I never see my family now."

She shot her fingers out one by one, listing her many reasons for feeling the way she did. "First, children are to go to events several times a week for the church, and if they are in sports, they are gone even more. You're supposed to have family home evening and do church work on Mondays, but isn't doing work for the church what Sunday afternoons are for? You're supposed to do temple work, which is weekly, and you are gone for hours. So, those who work outside of the home are either doing church work or their job all week. For example, on Mondays, you talk about the family home evening, attending the presidency meetings on Tuesday, Wednesday leaving for the temple to volunteer, prepare most events or lessons on Saturday, and then Sunday is church all day. Then, add reading scriptures every night, prayers in the morning, prayers at night, and prayers at meals. Might I also note that this doesn't include all the times that my husband is gone."

She paused briefly and looked up at the bishop, fully expecting him to chime in, then continued.

"Plus, you're supposed to give 10 percent of your earnings to the church, and it will provide blessings. Why be required to give a percentage? Why can't I give what I think is fair or can afford? And you know what? Life is rough, why can't I have a glass of wine on those days? Jesus did in the Bible, after all."

She stopped and sighed. The bishop's face was full of shock and awe. He took a breath and was silent, even though she handed him a printed copy of her list for their discussion.

Instead, he looked at Chelsea and asked, "You are the top woman leader in this church, right?"

"Yes, that is correct. *You* had the vision to put me over the women in this church ward," Chelsea declared, matching his tone of passive-aggressiveness.

The bishop then looked at his clock, "Well, sometimes you need to not wonder, and listen and follow your priesthood holders."

Chelsea tilted her head and looked at him questioningly. "Are you telling me that the answer to my questions is not to ask questions but to have faith in men?"

"That is correct, sister. Pray about it, and the answers will come," he stated, ushering her out the door. "I'm running late for another appointment now."

"Another appointment?" she gasped, turning on him. "Sir, how am I supposed to have faith in men like yourself if you can't even keep the time you've promised me to discuss my questions?"

He stood flabbergasted by her words as she continued. "If you are going to be a leader, then lead, and don't give me cop-out answers like 'men are always right.'"

She put on her coat and excused herself.

"There might be proof that says otherwise, but I am sure I'm in a cult," she said to herself on the way home.

LATER THAT NIGHT, SHE talked to Aaron's mom. "I am all about following what I see and feel is right. I am still giving 110% to my calling, in my temple work, the church, doing family home evening, my prayers, learning the scriptures, and serving others. But I feel that this is more of an obligation and not service done out of love. I don't feel that the church is all about love. I hate this feeling. I resent working full time, going to school full time, and stopping everything for church work, too. I'm always gone. My husband is always gone, and so are my children. I want to have two more children, but I feel like it will push me over the edge."

Her mother-in-law folded her arms as she pursed her lips. "Just quit school and work. The Lord is the most important."

Chelsea internally laughed at the suggestion. She was still the breadwinner of their home. There was no way she could give up work, and she'd be damned if she gave up school when she was so close to finishing.

After contemplating her life, she decided she needed to finish school before she had another baby. She was determined to finish her BS degree because she wanted two more children close in age. She already felt wrong about the age gap of four years between Tabby and Mace, and there would be a significant gap with future children. She knew if she waited too much longer, the new baby would feel like an only child.

That is assuming I can have another baby. Of course, then she was reminded of her reoccurring dreams that she'd had before, dreams with babies and children's laughter. She knew, somehow, that there was a little boy up in heaven waiting on her.

Chapter 27
THE DIVINE SEQUENCE OF NUMBERS

*C*HELSEA FELT THE PLUMERIAS tickling her bare feet as she was on a park bench talking to a little boy. He had red hair that stuck up straight up as if it wanted to touch the sky. His deep-set blue eyes twinkled and bounced as he talked. He had a little button nose with freckles all over it.

Their conversation was light and carefree as they discussed heaven and earth. Chelsea was impressed by how this little boy was so precise, brimming with intellectual genius. There was a way that he smiled, a warmth, a softness of spirit that she couldn't get over. They listened to one another as if they were absorbing each other's words.

After hours of talking, a thought danced over Chelsea as she asked him, "Are you going to be my son?"

In a triumphant voice, he said, "Yes."

Chelsea beamed at him as she hugged him goodbye. She sat on the bench, watching him as he walked and then disappeared. Just then, she felt a splatter of rain.

Beep! Beep! Beep! She turned and looked at the clock. "Wow, I must have missed my first alarm. It is already 10:30 A.M. I can't remember the last time I slept in that long."

She jumped out of bed and gasped when she saw the sheets drenched in blood. Her heart started to race as she rushed to the phone. "Aaron, come home! I think I'm losing the baby. I'm bleeding," Chelsea screamed frantically into the phone. She had tears rolling down her face as a sickening fear swirled through her.

"Chels, I'm on my way. Lie down, and I'll be there soon," Aaron stammered as he dropped the phone, and she heard the door swing open through the other end. He had clearly left work without hanging up, but Chelsea couldn't think about that. All she could think about was how long it would take him to drive home and then take her to the ER.

She continued to look at the clock, waiting impatiently for him to get home. At 10:37 A.M., she moved to lay on her left side and started drinking water.

I can't lose another baby. I dreamt about him earlier this week, and I saw that same number—1037—but bleeding like this isn't normal at all.

To distract herself from the pain and bleeding, she pulled up her computer and searched for those numbers, the ones she had seen in her dreams, and consistently on the clock. She clicked on the first link, which was Joanne Walmsley's Sacred Scribes blog:

ANGEL NUMBER 1037

Number 1037 is a combination of the attributes and energies of number 1 and number 0 and the vibrations and influences of number 3 and number 7. Number 1 brings with it the vibrations of self-leadership and assertiveness, initiative, instinct and intuition, new beginnings, and a fresh approach, motivation, striving forward, and progress. Number 1 reminds us that we create our own realities with our thoughts, beliefs, and actions. Number 0 is the number of the Universal Energies/ Source, the beginning point, eternity, infinity, oneness, wholeness, continuing cycles, and flow, developing one's spiritual aspects, and connecting with the higher-self, and it denotes freedom from limitations. Number 0 also amplifies the energies of the numbers it appears with. Number 3 is related to growth and expansion, affability, enthusiasm, spontaneity and broadmindedness, optimism and joy, natural talent and skills, creativity, manifesting your desires, self-expression, and communication. Number 3 is also associated with the energies of the Ascended Masters. Number 7 resonates with understanding the self and others, spiritual awakening and development, the empathic and psychic abilities. Angel Number 1037 is a message of congratulations from your angels and the Ascended Masters, for you have chosen the right course of action and are traveling well along your life path.

HER RELIGION DIDN'T BELIEVE in reincarnation or past lives, but she had seen and experienced enough to know that she had

had previous lives. She was an old soul. That is what made her so wise and strong.

"God, please help me to know what to do. Please bless this baby and my health. I will readily take his place if you require me to do so. Please help," she pleaded through her tears while she waited for Aaron.

After a few minutes of prayer, tears, and breathing, Chelsea went into the bathroom, and the bleeding had stopped. She looked up at the clock and saw 11:11 A.M.

"Well, it is official, God does listen to me," she sighed out loud as she heard Aaron bolting in the house.

"The car is running. Let's go!" He exclaimed.

"Aaron, it's okay. Trust me. I feel okay, and it will be okay. We can calm down now," she said as she was ushered into the car.

They drove to the emergency room, and the nurses were prompt in wheeling her back to an examination room. They immediately put an IV in her hand as they began going over her medical history.

"I had cervical cancer cells last year and had a few treatments. They had said this would be a high-risk pregnancy, but next to the bleeding this morning, it has gone well, and the baby has been rather healthy," Chelsea explained.

Her doctor walked into the room with the ultrasound machine. He smeared gel on her belly before pressing the device to her stomach.

"Oh, thank God! I hear the heartbeat," she cried out loud when she heard the same racehorse galloping that she had heard in her previous pregnancies.

The doctor looked at her. "He is still solid and healthy. Likely, your cervix was bleeding. It was thin after all of the treatments last year. Let's clamp the little guy in until it is time. He needs a little more time before he'll be ready to see the world."

Chelsea sighed loudly. Her worried tears turned into happy tears as she talked to her protruding belly, saying, "That's right, little Carter, you hang tight and stop trying to escape early."

Chapter 28
THE JOYS OF MOTHERHOOD

⸺

*I*T WAS TAX DAY, and Chelsea was dreading going to Tabby's maturation class. She left work around lunchtime and was grateful to leave early because she started to feel a migraine coming on. Chelsea knew that if she hurried home in time, she could take some medicine and get a few minutes of sleep before the meeting at Tabby's school.

I need to get home. The migraine is in the orb-seeing stage, so I can still prevent the big one.

After her last email to assign tasks to her staff, she could tell that words weren't coming quickly. *I feel so out of it. It is like you forget how to spell dog—your brain doesn't work. Thank God I now live five minutes away from work.* She looked in the rear-view mirror, noticing her vision was getting blurry.

She ran into the house and immediately ran to the medicine cabinet. She took two pills with a full glass of water, grabbed frozen peas from the freezer, and set the alarm for thirty-five minutes. She laid down on the bed with the peas on top of her head. "Please make the migraine go away so I can make it to Tabby's school," she prayed.

As she was lying on the bed, she couldn't believe that Carter had been in such a hurry to get out months ago, but now that the clamp had been removed and he could come out, he wouldn't. "He is taking his dear, sweet time. I didn't even get a break from tax season."

She giggled at the irony of her luck. "Only *I* would have a baby due during tax time and still not get a break during that time. At least I only have three more days of work, and then I get six weeks off of work," she exclaimed.

Beep! Beep! Beep! The alarm went off and startled Chelsea.

"I must have actually fallen asleep, but damn, my head hurts," she said as she was standing up slowly and began walking to the bathroom.

She looked in the mirror and said, "Oh, good, the orbs are gone, but the headache is full force. A headache during the maturation class. Sounds about right."

She headed out the door to drive to the school, which was thirty minutes away.

I am grateful my in-laws let us live with them for a month or two, but boy, this loud household has made resting nearly impossible. Not ideal when you are pregnant but so typical of how it goes.

Chelsea struggled to get out of the car and continued to hold the peas on her head. She locked the door, threw the keys in her purse, and then sighed, "I'm still holding the peas. Clearly, I'm having a day, and I can't think straight." She stuffed the peas into her purse and rushed into the school.

She entered the classroom and sat next to her daughter as she looked around. The windows cast squares on the white walls as the sun beamed in the room. There was a podium in the front of the room with a projector screen strategically placed next to it. Chelsea sighed, knowing that she would have to watch a presentation under the florescent lights.

She heard a loud sigh from Tabby. She glanced over to see Tabby giving her a disgusted look. "You look horrible. Why is half of your hair wet? I should have had my stepmom come."

Chelsea didn't say a word as Tabby moved a seat away from her. Chelsea shook her head. She had no energy and felt too horrible to chastise Tabby on her behavior and comments.

You might think I'm not the ideal parent, but you certainly are not the perfect child," Chelsea sighed as she felt her nose flaring at the thought of how someone so horrible could come out of her body.

Tabby can be here by herself. I don't need her abuse. I feel like hell. I'm nine months pregnant, took off work, and drove thirty minutes to support the brat. Her head was spinning, and she was gathering her things to go to the car when a girl pounced down beside her and hugged her tight. It was Alexis, a young teenager Chelsea had in her church class the year prior.

She smiled, touched Chelsea's belly, and exclaimed, "Oh my gosh, Chelsea, you look so cute pregnant. I was hoping you would be here because my mom couldn't make it, and I didn't want my dad to come."

Chelsea smiled and gushed, "You can be my daughter anytime. Thank you. He is due any day now."

Tabby looked over, glared, and hissed to Alexis, "Yes, why don't you be her daughter?"

"Yes, Alexis, you can be my daughter. I could use a polite and sweet daughter like you. You are an absolute joy to be around," Chelsea stated, ignoring Tabby.

"I would love to be with you all the time. You are lucky, Tabby," Alexis said matter-of-factly.

Tabby rolled her eyes and said, "She isn't all that."

Alexis gave her a puzzled but appalled look and turned back to Chelsea. "So, it's a boy?" Chelsea smiled and nodded as the speaker walked into the class.

Chelsea felt like the entire class was a blur, and she was relieved when it was over. They drove to pick up Mace from school and started to head home.

Tabby demanded, "Aren't we going to stop for something to eat?"

Chelsea glared at her and continued driving.

After the third time of asking, Tabby's tone was full of entitlement. Chelsea blew up and yelled, "We are going straight home. You are a disrespectful little shit. You can get something there and go to bed. I've had enough of you today."

Chelsea opened her purse and put the peas on the dashboard of the car and snapped, "Here, you can eat these if you are hungry now."

Tabby muttered under her breath, "Bitch."

Chelsea pulled the car over and screamed, "Tabby, get in the back or walk home!"

Tabby threw the door open, got out, slammed it, and jumped in the back. Chelsea continued to drive faster as tears started rolling down her cheeks.

Mace was only 8 years old, but was perspective enough to know that his mom was upset, said, "Guess what mom? I turned in all of my missing assignments today."

"Oh, wow! Good job, buddy. Let's try and turn them in the first time, and you won't have to redo them. Okay?"

AFTER FORTY-FIVE MINUTES OF driving, they finally arrived at home. Chelsea walked in the door and could smell food. She turned the corner and saw that her in-laws had dinner prepared. Chelsea looked surprised and cried, "Oh my! Thank you so much for making dinner tonight."

Aaron's mom smiled and said, "Well, I figured with Tax Day, going to Tabby's school, and being nine months pregnant, you might need a little break today."

Chelsea nodded and hugged her. Still, on the brink of tears, she turned and asked, "Would you be offended if I go and take a bath? I don't feel like eating tonight. I've been fighting a migraine."

She pulled the peas out of her purse and put them in the garbage. "I didn't have any ice packs, so I used these on my head, but I'll go shopping for some tomorrow."

Aaron's mom smiled and nodded. She then turned to her grandchildren. "Tabby and Mace, into the kitchen to eat. Let's give your mom a break tonight."

CHELSEA WAS LEANING BACK in the bath with tears rolling down her cheeks. She didn't raise Tabby the last twelve years to be so rude and disrespectful. Without a doubt, some of it had to do with Freddy. He had started to come into the kids' lives regularly as soon as she had married Aaron.

All of a sudden, she felt a sharp pain in her back. Chelsea cried as she tried to get up and found that she couldn't. The water began turning pink as blood started to flow into the bathwater.

"Help!" she called out several times with no answer.

She started to count the contractions and knew she needed to get out of the bath immediately.

She took a few deep breaths and pulled herself up, using the faucet spout. She tore the spout out of the wall, but she was up. She threw on her clothes, grabbed her overnight bag, and waddled up the stairs with the towel underneath her.

"My water broke, and I'm having close contractions," she exclaimed as she saw everyone eating. No one moved, and she turned her gaze to Aaron. "We have to go. Now!"

Aaron grabbed bread, his phone and ran to the car and jumped in.

Chelsea sighed. "You realize that your nine-month-pregnant wife is holding the overnight bag and walking with fluid coming out, right?" But Aaron didn't hear her and stayed in the car. He looked up to see her giving him a dirty look as she motioned for him to come and get the bag from her so that she could hold on to the railing while walking down a couple of steps.

On their way to the hospital, Chelsea called her mom to meet them. When they arrived at the hospital, the contractions were one minute apart and intense. She never even made it to the room. Instead, at 10:37 P.M., Carter was welcomed to the world in the hospital's hallway.

Chapter 29
SHE IS BETTER OFF DEAD

CARTER WAS HER MIRACLE child. Even the nurse seemed to think so, commenting, "There is something about him, that's for sure," as she helped Chelsea with her hospital discharge papers.

Arriving home from the hospital should have been a joy, but instead, it was more like a three-dimensional mess. Tabby walked in the door with a chip on her shoulder and opted to remain silent and glared at the new baby. Being around Tabby was like walking on eggshells, which made Chelsea disgusted, and it was getting to the point that Chelsea was seriously considering putting her in military school.

TABBY'S PRE-TEEN ATTITUDE IMPROVED slightly when Aaron and Chelsea announced they would be moving that week, but no one was more excited than Chelsea, who was glad their new place would be more spacious and provide some privacy for the five family members.

She had already started buying decorations for the children's rooms and was excited to put it all together. Tabby wanted her room Hawaiian, so Chelsea bought a Hawaiian bed skirt, a fishnet canopy, mural wallpaper, a palm tree, window coverings that would make it look like she was looking out into the ocean, and bedding and accessories that tied everything together.

Mace wanted his room to be camping themed, so Chelsea bought a tent she could put on top of a bed and put his mattress inside of it, lights for the tent, and a wood stump as a nightstand. A mural of the outdoors covered an entire wall. Chelsea even added some 4 feet pine trees as accessories.

Chelsea was still trying to figure out what to do with Carter's room, but she was thinking of cars or trains.

Growing up, Chelsea's family had worked hard to give her what she needed, but they certainly didn't have the money to give her what she wanted. Her clothes were sometimes handme-downs from cousins and her sister, but she was always grateful for anything she had because she knew the value of her parent's hard work.

Compared to her childhood, Tabby and Mace were living the high life, yet they often complained they had a hard time with her working all the time or, paradoxically, with her being home too much and bothering them about homework or coming home by their curfew. She couldn't appease her two eldest children no matter what she did.

It seemed to her that the critical difference between her and her oldest children was that she appreciated her parents' sacrifices, and Tabby and Mace had no clue and didn't care to notice Chelsea's.

Maybe their own space, privacy, and serenity will help with their treatment of everyone around them, Chelsea thought as she looked down and smiled at Carter.

"Please be nothing like them. Please make me feel like my sacrifices are worth it in your eyes," she whispered as he looked up at her with big, wide eyes.

"WHERE ARE MY CHILDREN?" Chelsea yelled, calling their names over and over as she envisioned them complaining about the food being cold. Only two houses down, she heard squeals, so she picked up Carter and ventured off to see if two of those squeals belonged to Tabby and Mace.

She peered into the neighbor's backyard to see the children running around with Nerf guns and screaming. Mace looked over and groaned upon meeting his mother's eyes, knowing it was time to come home. Tabby looked over and rolled her eyes. Then she continued to talk to a teenage boy who was also in the yard.

Chelsea motioned for them to come home. The neighbor came out and began to talk to her. She was an older woman with blonde hair and a hardened look. Still, she was pleasant enough and stated, "I'll be calling my boys in now as well." After a moment, she said, "Welcome to the neighborhood," and she took a moment to meet Chelsea and coo at Carter.

"Thank you. It's good to be moved in," Chelsea stated as Carter began to fuss. "Please excuse us. I need to feed him and the other two in the back," she said, motioning toward her children.

Twenty minutes later, Tabby and Mace came barreling in, asking, "What's for dinner?"

Chelsea, burping Carter, pointed to the table. "You'll have to heat it up now because it's gotten cold." Tabby rolled her eyes, and Chelsea couldn't help feeling the ungratefulness spread.

Chelsea walked out of the room to avoid going postal. *I can't wait for her to have a child like her! I'm done cooking meals and preparing for us all to eat. It is a lost cause.*

She sat down on the couch to take a breather, and soon Mace was right there next to her, shoveling spoonfuls of food into his mouth. He looked over at Chelsea. "Did you know that Tabby shares a birthday with the neighbor boy, Ethan?"

"Oh, really? That's cool," Chelsea said, smiling because he was actually engaging in conversation. She took a clean corner of the burp rag and wiped some food off Mace's chin.

"Mom!" he declared, annoyed. Chelsea smiled, and he kept eating.

"So, how do you know that?" Chelsea asked.

"Tabby and Ethan were talking, and I guess they were born the same day, hours apart, and in the same hospital," Mace continued, proud he was engaging in grown-up talk.

"Talk about a coincidence!" Chelsea exclaimed as she went back into the kitchen to pull brownies from the oven. She served Mace a brownie as a reward for his excellent behavior.

SHE COULDN'T STOP FALLING. She kept screaming and reaching for the cliff, which was filled with plumerias. *Why am I falling in fast motion over and over past the same cliff and never landing?* She felt an endless panic rise within her. Weird memories and flashbacks of her life appeared before her in slow motion.

She abruptly found herself in a meadow and began walking. She could hear cackling and people talking. She walked toward the sound and saw Tabby sitting on a bench with Ethan.

They both looked over and saw her and began whispering to one another, laughing and pointing at her. "She won't know what hit her," she heard Ethan say.

"She's better off dead," Tabby replied back with jealous and evil eyes.

Chelsea felt her heartbreak inside into a million pieces, and her soul writhed in agony.

"You know I hear you plotting to kill me, right? Nothing will ever teach you if you don't let the light in. How many lives are you going to repeat this evil cycle?" Chelsea yelled to her daughter, her arms out, blocking the darkness that surrounded them as she tried to free a hand and extend it out to Tabby. Around Chelsea, a light began to spread.

"Bitch!" Tabby rebuked, and she and Ethan began to back away, further into the darkness.

She heard a male voice. "Chelsea, it will be okay. You have a good heart!"

She looked around. "Who said that? What does that mean?" she exclaimed.

BEEP! BEEP! BEEP! THE alarm sounded, and Chelsea rolled out of bed and onto her feet. She was so tired she didn't hear Aaron leave earlier, but today was her first day back to work. She was going back part-time because she desperately wanted to spend more time with Carter and, believe it or not, Mace and Tabby. Still, there was something about Carter that made her feel like he was literally an angel on earth.

She quickly fed Carter and got him ready for the day, a feat that would have taken three times as long when Tabby and Mace were little, before begrudgingly heading downstairs to wake up said little monsters.

Mace was first, and as she entered his room, she took a moment to look at him with a bit of envy. The position he was in looked uncomfortable, but the deep snores and awkwardness revealed a depth of sleep that Chelsea didn't think she'd ever experienced. It was, in a way, beautiful. She pushed the off button to his alarm clock and reminded him that school was starting soon, so he needed to get up.

Once he was in at least a semi-upright position, Chelsea went to wake Tabby. Tabby cursed at her, but she eventually got up when Chelsea told her if she gave her any more sass and difficulty, Tabby would leave without breakfast.

AT WORK, THE DAY flew by, and it was as if she had never left. She had been nervous that morning because she was coming back part-time with a new baby at home, but now everything seemed fine.

It helped that Aaron had decided to work for his family's company so she could be at home and not working all the time.

There now was enough financial support in the household that Chelsea felt like she could breathe. It was a luxury she had never had in the past, and she planned to take full advantage of it.

Plus, her boss, Dan, was always so sweet and asked about the marriage, move, baby, religion, and everything else. One thing about Dan was that no matter where she was in life, he seemed to remember and take an interest in her well-being.

BEFORE SHE KNEW IT, it was time to go home, but instead of the four hours of work, it had been six.

"Well, some things don't change. I can never escape," she joked as she rushed to get Carter from the babysitter.

THAT NIGHT, CHELSEA TOSSED and turned, but finally surrendered to sleep.

SHE COULD SMELL THE earth she walked on—each step brought a different fragrance. It was an earthy smell of soil stirred by the thrust of grass stems. The aroma reminded her of flowers that had just been rained upon. She knew she was in a dream but felt at peace and kept walking through the meadow. She wiped the tears off her cheeks, knowing it was residue from her waking state.

I can hear people talking. She walked toward the voices. She recognized the voices but couldn't figure out who they were. She continued to walk and walk and walk.

How can I hear voices, but not find the people talking?

She looked over, saw plumerias, and picked one up to take with her on her walk. She saw a bench and sat down to rest from the hours of walking. Suddenly, someone tapped her on the shoulder, and she turned around to see a young woman. The woman was beautiful, with dark, curly hair, flawless skin, and a slender build.

"Hi!" Chelsea said.

"Follow me," the woman insisted as she started to walk.

They walked across a bridge where she saw people gathered. A gentleman walked over to greet them and murmured, "Hello, Chelsea!"

The older man had grey hair around his balding, mottled scalp. His back was slightly hunched. Chelsea could see how his worry lines crossed with his smile lines.

Chelsea smiled at him. "I recognize your voice, but do I know you?"

He returned the smile. "You do!" He touched her arm and declared, "Not everything you see, will you know. Trust your heart, and do not let life harden it." He pulled another plumeria from the ground and handed it to Chelsea before he walked away.

Chelsea looked around, and everyone had left her in the field alone. She sat, wondering what it all meant. How did she know this old man? Just then heard something in the distance. *Is that a baby crying? Wake up, Chelsea, it might be Carter needing you.*

Sure enough, Carter was waking her. As she picked him up and began to rock him, she couldn't help but tell him about her bizarre dream and the odd message. "'Not everything you see, will you know,' Um, okay? At this point, I don't know anything and have seen a lot," she whispered to Carter, who smiled at his mother's voice.

TABBY CONTINUED TO ACT up in school, and it seemed to get worse the more she was around Ethan and his family. Mace was still struggling in school, but at least he was turning in his assignments on time.

And when it seemed things couldn't get worse, Aaron came home and declared, "Baby! My parents are selling the business, so I'll be without a job soon."

Chelsea looked at him, confused. "Wait! Why would your parents do that? That doesn't make sense at all. You run the entire thing, and they have been still making money."

Aaron struggled and stammered, "I guess they were done with it."

Chelsea knew Aaron was lying when she began getting migraines from every conversation they had about work, which led her to do some snooping. Sure enough, Aaron had lied when he said that the family was selling their generations-old business, leaving him unemployed. In fact, he had quit, and that was why they were selling the business.

I have to go back to working full time while dealing with family drama. My life is spiraling out of control again.

Chelsea didn't want the kids to know how much they were financially impaired, which was because of Aaron quitting his job. Once again, it was up to her to carry the financial weight for their family. She was angry that Aaron had put all of that pressure back on her again. And why? Because he "didn't like working on weekends."

She needed Jessica to vent to. She picked up the phone and called her.

"My Prince Charming is turning into all the others. He's lying to me about his job and who knows what else. What is wrong with me? Do I expect too much?" Chelsea asked Jessica.

Jessica, as usual, successfully pulled her off of her metaphorical ledge, and they both took turns venting and consoling one another in their marriages.

A WEEK LATER, CHELSEA walked in the front door from work, exhausted and wanting nothing more than to go straight to Carter for a hug and kiss. Aaron was in the garage cleaning his golf clubs, so she made a beeline for Carter's crib, but he was nowhere to be seen.

She went back to the garage, annoyed, and asked, "Where is Carter?"

Aaron replied, "Oh, I gave him to your mom earlier. I went golfing today."

It blew Chelsea's mind that he could go golfing while she spent more than twelve hours working.

"How's that job hunt coming?" Chelsea snapped.

"I'm learning how to flip homes now. I went through some courses and set up a few meetings with a couple of people," Aaron replied, oblivious to Chelsea's rising temper.

"Okay, let me see if I understand. You spent, what, an hour or two taking a course online on how to flip houses, then decided you've learned enough to know how to do it and said, Screw it, I'm going to play golf all day and leave my baby with the in-laws, *again?*" Chelsea hissed.

Aaron stopped polishing his clubs and quickly packed them away.

"Oh, my hell! Grow up, Aaron," she said as she jumped into her car.

While driving, she picked up her cell phone and called her parents to let them know she'd be picking up Carter shortly. She still had several things left on her list of things to do—dinner, clean up the living room, help Mace with his homework, care for the baby, and try to finish some church work. Half of those things Aaron was supposed to have done while she was at work.

When she picked up Carter, her spirit felt a little better. Just seeing his face seemed to relieve her of some of her anger toward Aaron.

"Mom, dad, you know how much I appreciate you babysitting him, but with Aaron quitting his job, please make him step up and at least watch Carter. That way, he won't spend the day golfing and playing while I work my ass off. This is the fourth time in two weeks he's done it, and I really think a bit of tough love will help him grow up," Chelsea said, hugging Carter into her chest.

Her mom smiled and sighed. "You are right. He needs to learn that he has more things around the house, or he'll have to go to work quicker." Her dad stoically nodded behind her.

"Thanks for understanding," she told them before heading home.

Of course, even with the extra time she had provided Aaron by going to pick up Carter, Aaron had failed to prepare dinner, meaning that Chelsea was bombarded by two hangry children when she arrived home.

"What's for dinner?" Mace and Tabby repeatedly yelled, as though the repetition would make her respond faster.

"I don't know, ask your dad. I barely walked in the door," she replied, making a beeline for the bedroom with Carter in tow.

Moments later, Aaron walked into the bedroom and asked, "I need to make dinner?"

Chelsea gave a tight smile and spat, "Oh, I don't know, Aaron. I worked for twelve hours and had to go get the baby. I assumed you already had."

Aaron walked out of the room, knowing Chelsea was ready to blow up. He started tasking Tabby and Mace with cleaning up their rooms as he pulled out some pots and pans.

Chapter 30
WHY NOT LIVE A LITTLE?

"I NEED YOU TO LOOK at this, Chels! This is the home we're buying," Aaron said, smiling.

Chelsea looked at the computer screen with worry. "Can we afford that? I think not," she said as she pulled away from the computer.

Aaron scoffed. "Yes, we can. They will use our credit for one home, and we will get forty thousand dollars on the flip. Since it's by Disney World, we can go and stay there on vacation while I fix it up at night. It will be good for the kids, and it will give you the vacation you need. The real question is, do you think you could get off work for a week?"

Chelsea smiled as she looked back at the computer screen. Maybe it was the exhaustion, but for some reason, she believed him.

"I definitely need to get some time off of work, or I'm going to lose some vacation time. I'm at the point where either I use it or lose it, so I'm sure I can get off," she mused. "Still—"

"Chels, this will be fine. I promise. Plus, it will be good for your employees to take on responsibilities instead of relying on you. The kids definitely need time with us, too, since you're working all the time, and I've been locked in the office doing the prep work for buying the property."

Chelsea closed her eyes and gave it some more profound thought. She did feel like she was always working, and she would love to spend a little time with the kids now that she was back to work more than forty hours a week.

"Fine. If you really think so, let's do it," she exclaimed. *Why not live a little?*

Aaron bounced up. He planted a kiss on her on the cheek before leaving the room.

"Guess what kids, we're going to Disney World!" she heard him exclaim down the hall before hearing cheers from Mace and Tabby, then a squeal from Carter, who joined in the excitement without knowing what he was cheering for.

ONCE THEY ARRIVED IN Florida, the children were beaming at the thoughts of riding rides and seeing all of the Disney characters. It made Chelsea happy to see that her children were finally excited about something and didn't have an attitude or complaint. In fact, thus far, it was all smiles and sunny days as they settled into a vacation frame of mind.

As promised, the condo was close to Disney World, and the day they arrived. Aaron and Chelsea were able to close the deal and sign the necessary documents to buy the property. Chelsea was adamant that the closing was going to be done as soon as they arrived. She wasn't going to torture her children on vacation by going to a title company for hours to sign documents. The company wanted the closing, and so they obliged, sending a representative to meet them at the local pool and finishing it all up within an hour.

For the first time in a while, Chelsea felt like she could breathe again. As she looked around to see the kids' smiling faces, she declared, "I could live here."

Aaron laughed, and she did, too, but after a minute or two, it seemed like she had an epiphany. "I mean, I never wanted to stay in Utah, but then children changed the whole plan of leaving Utah. Having a home here . . . it's a good alternative. Maybe we could rent the place after we clean it up instead of selling it, you know?"

Aaron nodded in agreement as she sat there, watching the children in the pool with Carter asleep on her lap.

The next day, they spent hours at Disney, and it was as if everything was aligned with their family. Tabby's attitude was gone, Mace seemed to be less whiny, and Carter was still the sweetest baby.

Finally, a happy family moment with no drama or stress. She sighed as the sun warmed her legs, which peeked out from beyond the umbrella's shadow.

"Thank you, baby. I really needed this," she gushed, kissing Aaron. "We really needed this."

Chapter 31
TO RISE AGAIN

―⌒―

"I CAN'T BELIEVE HE NEVER got to see the picture," Chelsea sobbed out loud to herself, as she was driving home in tears after picking up a drawing she had commissioned for her boss, Robert. "I orchestrated a picture to cheer him up as he battled cancer, and he didn't even see it. I missed him by one damn day," she cried, looking at the picture of the five buildings that housed the company and his image raising above the middle of them. She wanted so badly to surprise him with a card from all of the employees and this beautiful drawing.

SHE DROPPED OFF THE picture to her boss's son, Dan.

"I'm so sorry for your loss," Chelsea said in a meek voice. "We had this done for him. It is all of the places the company worked from with a sketch of him, the founder."

"He died in my arms, but he's no longer suffering," Dan whispered, holding the picture with tears in his eyes. "You are always so thoughtful. You always know what to say and do. This will look amazing at the funeral, and my mom will love it." He hugged her and looked at the card before closing it. "Hey, wait, I thought today was your day off."

"It is my day off, and I'm off to get the kids from school to go to my dad's house. He is having knee surgery today, but I wanted to drop off the picture, even if it is late," she explained, smiling sadly.

"Well, it is good to see you, but go enjoy the day off. You certainly don't have many," he said.

"Please let me know if I can do anything," she replied, walking out the door.

She tried to pull herself together before she picked up the children from school. Carter was in the back seat, drifting off to sleep, and she still needed to go to the store for balloons and a card before they went to see Chelsea's dad after his knee surgery.

At the store, they were looking at all of the balloons when Mace spotted a singing balloon that had a big smiley face on it. "We are getting this one," he declared.

"This one sings, 'Don't Worry, Be Happy,'" he told his mom, and Chelsea laughed as Carter began grabbing for the balloon.

"Well, grandpa will love that balloon," Chelsea giggled.

They left and made their way to her parent's home. The children were instantly angels around their grandpa, showering him with the get-well cards they had made and the singing balloon.

Tabby was frantically going through her school bag to find a second handmade card with a drawing she had done on it herself. "I can't find the other card I made him. I must have left it at home," she sobbed.

"That's okay! We can give it to him tomorrow," Chelsea insisted.

Tabby threw down her school bag in a rage. "But I want him to have it now!"

Chelsea took another of many deep breathes that day and sighed. "Well, sweetheart, grandpa needs to rest. We'll stop by tomorrow and give it to him."

Tabby stomped her foot like a toddler and stormed off to complain to her grandpa, who told her the same thing Chelsea had. "Your mom is right, and you need to listen to her. I will get the card tomorrow when you come to visit me. I can't wait to see what you drew on it."

Chelsea knew her mom's hands were full, taking care of her dad. As they started to prepare dinner, her mother vented to her. "They sent him home with an oxygen tank for such a low oxygen level, and he was too stubborn to stay the night in the hospital. He is so bull-headed. He has never been in the hospital overnight and was even born on the kitchen table. It looks like I'm the at-home nurse."

Chelsea shook her head and responded, "The hospital stay would have been good for him. Although I do understand wanting to be in his own bed. I hope they talked to him about losing weight, too."

"Yes, they did, and his heart was causing them concern, but he passed the EKG. He will get the chemical stress tests tomorrow, so we need to go back to the hospital early tomorrow morning—don't get me started," her mom grumbled, shaking her head at the amount of stubbornness her husband of thirty-seven years had.

Chelsea uttered, "Well, we'll be back tomorrow to help out, and we will bring Tabby's card. You know, she really is an amazing artist, and she was at the kitchen table working on it for a while. Tabby is so difficult, and I've had a hell of a day. My boss, Robert, died last night, and the picture I was working on for him didn't get to him in time. I missed it by one day. One day. Maybe I shouldn't have had it framed. At least then, he would have seen it."

Her mom patted her back, comfortingly. "Well, it will be perfect for the family at the funeral now."

Chelsea nodded, and they continued to make dinner.

As THEY WERE LEAVING, Chelsea took a final moment to size up her dad.

"It looks like we'll see you tomorrow, dad. For hell's sake, listen to the doctor and your wife," she remarked with a smile, "and keep the oxygen on for the night."

He looked over at her with the smirk on his face. "Maybe."

Chelsea, her mom, and Sadie all knew that *maybe* in their family, usually meant it wasn't going to happen.

She hugged her dad and kissed him goodbye. "You are a stubborn ass. Be good, and I'll see you tomorrow," she blurted with a matching smirk.

"That smirk and attitude! God, I love it and yet hate it,"

she groaned loud enough for him to hear as she walked out the door. Behind her, she heard a roaring laugh.

CHELSEA WENT INTO THE office early the next morning to ensure she was not needed. It was two weeks after tax season, and with the added tragedy of the company's legacy dying the day before, she knew it was going to be a slow day. She still couldn't wrap her head around poor Robert being gone. After nine years of seeing his face at work, it felt odd not to see him there.

She started to feel the tears well up, so she gathered her things to go back home.

When Chelsea felt vulnerable, she usually found it best to go into hermit mode. It was how she coped. She looked down at the clock and saw it was only 9:30 A.M., way too early to stay home. *Maybe I should go shopping while Carter is with Aaron and his family.* She headed to the grocery store.

She caved and bought some ice cream and then drove home, intending to eat half a tub of the sugary delight the minute she was home.

As she was unloading the groceries, Aaron drove into the driveway behind her. She saw Carter's red hair sticking up in the backseat.

"What are you doing here? I thought you were dropping Carter off to spend time with your mom." Chelsea wondered in a surprised but calm voice.

Aaron came up, hugged her, grabbed her shoulders, and pulled her away slightly to look into her eyes. "Chels, your dad just died."

Chelsea dropped the bag of groceries she was holding and looked at him in disbelief, shaking her head. "That is impossible!

I saw my dad yesterday. It was a scope on his knee. It's not major surgery. My dad was fine last night. He was even sarcastic and stubborn," she stammered. "You've made a mistake. He even had that smirk on his face and was giving me shit."

She bent down to pick up the bag she had dropped as tears rolled down her face. She knew Aaron hadn't made a mistake, and her knees buckled as she collapsed against the back bumper of her car. "You need to wake him up."

Aaron helped her up and ushered her into the backseat to sit with Carter, closing the trunk behind him.

She began to sob uncontrollably. "We are going to your mom's house now," Aaron told her as she leaned her head against Carter's seat and continued to cry.

CHELSEA WALKED INTO HER parent's house to find paramedics and the police there. She ran up to talk to her sister, who was upset and shaking.

"Did you try waking him up?" Chelsea asked, still attempting to convince herself this wasn't happening. "Maybe he is in a deep sleep."

Sadie shook her head, and Chelsea walked out of the room and found out the details of the morning. Sadie had tried CPR until she realized he had passed hours earlier.

"Chels, can you deal with the paramedics?" her mom asked as she, too, was visibly shaking. Chelsea nodded and walked the paramedics into his bedroom. She looked at her dad. His skin had a purplish-grey tint reminiscent of clay. His face was frozen, solid-looking, more like a statue than a body.

She looked as she saw his body sinking into the mattress, almost as though he was going to melt into the bed, *it's clear he is dead. There is no soul in that body. Oh my God, my dad is gone. I can't believe he is dead after a scrape on his knee.*

She felt an immediate presence come over her—the smell of her dad's cologne and a chill generating goosebumps all over her body. *He is here. I feel him. His spirit is hugging me.*

The tears stopped flowing, and she smiled and whispered, "Dad, I love you. Please go watch over mom and Sadie now. I'll be strong now."

Before she knew it, it was time to go and get the children from school. She excused herself to go pick them up.

Tabby jumped in first and sat in the front seat. When she looked at her mom, her brows furrowed and lips pursed as she asked, "What? What is wrong?" It wasn't in a caring tone, more sarcastic, but Chelsea didn't care at the moment.

"We will talk when we are at home," Chelsea replied slowly, trying to keep herself from falling apart.

Tabby rolled her eyes. "Whatever, as long as we get to see grandpa today."

Chelsea felt her heart shatter as it dropped into the pit of her stomach. Then Mace jumped in the car and started rambling about his day. He saw Carter in his car seat and began to play with him while chattering on. Carter was squealing with glee that his older brother was playing with him. Chelsea focused on that to get her through the drive home.

When Chelsea pulled into the garage, she asked, "Kids, can you go into the family room? I need to talk to you."

She had them all sit on the couch next to each other. Then she knelt down to be on the same level as them. She looked them in the eyes as she touched Tabby and Mace's knees, and she started to cry. It took her a few moments to gather herself again, and her children watched their mother's strange behavior with concern.

"Grandpa . . ." she said with a pause, "died this morning."

Both of them held blank expressions as she continued. "They don't know what happened yet, but he didn't wake up after he went to bed last night."

Mace immediately started to cry and buried his head in his hands.

Tabby burst into tears, shoving her mother's hand off of her knee. "He never got the card that I made him!" she blurted as she began to shake.

Chelsea put on a fake smile through her own tears. "Sweetheart, he can see it and is probably holding it as we speak from heaven," she cried, touching her daughter's knee again. "I don't know a lot of things, but I can say without a doubt that grandpa is in heaven and watching us."

Her voice was trembling now as the three of them cried.

After the sobs slowed, Chelsea rose to a stand. "Tabby, why don't you run downstairs and grab the card now? We will go over and see grandma and Aunt Sadie."

Tabby nodded and stood up to run downstairs. She came up the stairs a moment later with the card in her hand. "Here, mom. This is what I made."

Chelsea looked at the card, and as she turned it over, she burst into tears. Tabby looked at her mom, confused. "Why are you crying? Do you not like it?"

Chelsea hugged Tabby and motioned for her to sit down next to her on the couch. She read the title, *RISE AGAIN*, aloud. It was written over a sunset with mountains and a ray of sunshine.

Chelsea explained as tears rolled down her cheeks. "The phrase 'rise again' signifies when Jesus was to rise again and come back to life. You might have meant, rise out of bed, but an angel helped you write it because it shows the dead are not gone. Their souls will rise up. Grandpa might have left this world, but he is in heaven, and he will rise again."

Chelsea continued to read the card out loud: *Grandpa, get well soon! This card reminds me of you because, every summer, when we are at your house, you take me outside and show me the colors of the sunset. I don't just see the sunset. I see your wonderful smile, and that beats all. I love you.*

Tabby sobbed. "Do you think grandpa likes the card?"

Chelsea hugged her tight. "Oh, I know he does. You did a great job, sweetheart. This came from the heart, and I'm going to let you decide if you want to keep the card your scrapbook or if you want to put it with him in his casket, okay?"

Tabby nodded. "Okay. I might keep it. An angel helped me write it."

Acknowledgments

WRITING THIS BOOK WAS a lot harder than I ever thought it would be. It is based on real-life events of my struggles and triumphs. Each event had to be relived over and over until the story was written. I'm eternally grateful for all those who have helped me and loved me through it all.

My life has been filled with many ups and downs, but those painful lessons became part of the story.

Writing a book about the story of your life is a surreal process. I'm am forever indebted to Terri Hatch, Jennifer House, and Sean Linton for their editorial help and expertise. I would also like to express gratitude to Dayna Linton for her keen insight in making my stories into reality.

To Eva Lynn London, Shelly London, Connor Checketts, and Heather Flinders, thank you for always being the people I could turn to during my many dark and desperate years. You have sustained me, loved me, and cared for me in ways words cannot express.

Finally, to all those who have been a part of my getting here. I love and appreciate the good and bad examples that you were in my life. I live in forgiveness and without regrets.

About the Author

JYL LONDON IS THE mother of three. A passionate volunteer in charities. She is also happy to be called an IT Nerd and is the CEO of her own companies.

She does her best writing on the beach, overlooking a pool or barricaded in the home she shares with her youngest son, Connor Checketts, and her puppy, Arrow.

Jyl loves to dream of plumerias, mystical heroes, and a better world. She is also proof that women are stronger than they look. She hopes that chivalry is alive and well, somewhere, so she'll find her prince charming.